Demian

INTERNATIONAL BESTSELLERS

- Animal Farm by George Orwell
  Fiction/Classic, 128 pp, ISBN: 9789354993381
- Demian by Hermann Hesse
  Fiction/Classic, 176 pp, ISBN: 9789354993398
- How to Win Friends and Influence People by Dale Carnegie
  Self-Help/Relations, 248 pp, ISBN: 9789354993404
- My Inventions: The Autobiography of Nikola Tesla
  Autobiography, 112 pp, ISBN: 9789354990076
- Relativity by Albert Einstein
  Science/Physics, 176 pp, ISBN: 9789354990144
- Siddhartha by Hermann Hesse
  Fiction/Classic, 144 pp, ISBN: 9789354990267
- The Art of War by Sun Tzû
  Self-Help/Strategy, 112 pp, ISBN: 9789354990342
- The Diary of a Young Girl by Anne Frank
  Autobiography/Memoir, 240 pp, ISBN: 9789354990434
- The Little Prince by Antoine De Saint-Exupéry
  Children's/Classic, 112 pp, ISBN: 9789354990519
- The Power of Your Subconscious Mind by Joseph Murphy
  Self-Help/Success, 240 pp, ISBN: 9789354990557
- The Prophet by Kahlil Gibran
  Fiction/Classic, 112 pp, ISBN: 9789354990632
- The Richest Man in Babylon by George S. Clason
  Self-Help/Finance, 168 pp, ISBN: 9789354990717

Search the book by its ISBN

DEMIAN

HERMANN HESSE

Words Power
An Imprint of General Press

Words Power
An Imprint of General Press

4805/24, Fourth Floor, Krishna House
Ansari Road, Daryaganj, New Delhi - 110002
Ph : 011-23282971, 45795759
E-mail : generalpressindia@gmail.com

First Edition : 2022

ISBN : 9789354993398

Printed by Repro Books Limited

Contents

Introduction

First published in 1919, it is a brilliant journey of the psyche written by one of Germany's most influential writers and thinkers—Herman Hesse. A young man awakens to selfhood and a world of possibilities beyond the conventions of his upbringing. Emil Sinclair is a quiet boy drawn into a forbidden yet seductive realm of petty crime and deviance. His guide is his precocious, mysterious classmate Max Demian, who provokes in Emil a search for self-discovery and spiritual fulfillment.

Demian is a classic coming-of-age story that continues to inspire generations of readers in its exploration of good and evil, morality, and self-discovery.

About the Author

Hermann Hesse (b. 1877) was a German-born Swiss poet and author, best known for writing the novels 'Steppenwolf', 'Siddhartha', and 'The Glass Bead Game'. He was awarded the Nobel Prize for Literature in 1946. His themes focus on man's struggle to break away from the rigid structures of civilization and follow his essential and inner spirit. For this, Hesse became a literary cult figure.

Prologue

All I really wanted was to try and live the life that was spontaneously welling up within me. Why was that so very difficult?

To tell my story I have to start far in the past. If I could, I'd have to go back much farther yet, to the very earliest years of my childhood and even beyond them to my distant origins.

When authors write novels, they usually act as if they were God and could completely survey and comprehend some person's history and present it as if God were telling it to Himself, totally unveiled, in its essence at all points. I can't, anymore than those authors can. But my story is more important to me than any author's is to him, because it's my own; it's the story of a human being—not an invented, potential, ideal, or otherwise nonexistent person, but a real, unique, living one. To be sure, people today have less of an idea than ever before what a really living person is; in fact, human beings, each one of whom is a priceless, unique experiment of nature, are being shot to death in car-loads.[1] If we weren't something more than unique individuals, if we could really be totally dispatched from the world by a bullet, it would no longer make sense to tell stories. But each person is not only himself, he is also the unique, very special point, important and noteworthy in every instance, where the phenomena of

1. The First World War was still raging at the time of writing.

the world meet, once only and never again in the same way. And so every person's story is important, eternal, divine; and so every person, to the extent that he lives and fulfills nature's will, is wondrous and deserving of full attention. In each of us spirit has become form, in each of us the created being suffers, in each of us a redeemer is crucified.

Not many people nowadays know what man is. Many feel it and therefore die more easily, just as I shall die more easily when I have finished writing this story.

I have no right to call myself one who knows. I was one who seeks, and I still am, but I no longer seek in the stars or in books; I'm beginning to hear the teachings of my blood pulsing within me. My story isn't pleasant, it's not sweet and harmonious like the invented stories; it tastes of folly and bewilderment, of madness and dream, like the life of all people who no longer want to lie to themselves.

Every person's life is a journey toward himself, the attempt at a journey, the intimation of a path. No person has ever been completely himself, but each one strives to become so, some gropingly, others more lucidly, according to his abilities. Each one carries with him to the end traces of his birth, the slime and eggshells of a primordial world. Many a one never becomes a human being, but remains a frog, lizard, or ant. Many one is a human being above and a fish below. But each one is a gamble of Nature, a hopeful attempt at forming a human being. We all have a common origin, the Mothers,[2] we all come out of the same abyss; but each of us, a trial throw of the dice from the depths,

---

2. Perhaps merely "our mothers," but in view of the mythological nature of this novel, almost surely a reference to the "Mothers," primordial earth goddesses, in Acts One and Two of the Second Part of Goethe's Faust.

strives toward his own goal. We can understand one another, but each of us can only interpret ourselves.

CHAPTER 1

Two Worlds

I begin my story with an experience from the time I was ten years old and attending the grammar school[3] in our small town.

Many memories are wafted to me, touching me inwardly with melancholy and with pleasurable thrills: narrow, dark streets and bright houses and steeples, the chiming of clocks and people's faces, rooms filled with hominess and warm comfort, rooms filled with mystery and profound fear of ghosts. There is a smell of cozy confinement, of rabbits and servant girls, of home remedies and dried fruit. Two worlds coincided there, day and night issued from two poles.

One world was my father's house, but it was even more restricted than that: it actually comprised only my parents. For the most part, this world was very familiar to me; it meant mother and father, love and severity, exemplary manners and school.

3. Lateinschule, "a school in which Latin is taught," is sometimes synonymous with Gymnasium, sometimes, as here, with an elementary school that prepares talented and/or well-to-do children for the Gymnasium. In any case, it is contrasted with the Volksschule, the ordinary public elementary school.

This was the world of a warm glow, clarity, and cleanliness; gentle, friendly speech, washed hands, clean clothes, and proper behavior were at home here. Here the morning chorale was sung, here Christmas was celebrated. In this world there were straight lines and paths leading to the future, there was duty and guilt, a troubled conscience and confession, forgiveness and good resolutions, love and respect, Bible sayings and wisdom. This was the world to adhere to if one's life was to be bright and pure, lovely and well-ordered.

On the other hand, the other world began right in our own house; it was altogether different, smelled different, spoke differently, made different promises and demands. In this second world, there were maids and journeymen, ghost stories and scandalous rumors; there was a motley flow of uncanny, tempting, frightening, puzzling things, things like slaughterhouse and jail, drunks and bickering women, cows giving birth, horses collapsing, stories of burglaries, killings, suicides. All these beautiful and scary, wild and cruel things existed all around, in the next street, in the next house; policemen and vagrants ran around, drunks beat their wives, clusters of young girls poured out of the factories in the evening, old women could cast a spell on you and make you sick, bandits lived in the woods, arsonists were caught by the constabulary—this second, violent world gushed out flagrantly everywhere, except in our rooms, where Mother and Father were. And that was very good. It was wonderful that here among us there was peace, order, and repose, duty and a clear conscience, forgiveness and love—and wonderful that all the rest existed, all those noisy, glaring, somber, and violent things, which nevertheless could be escaped with a single bound toward one's mother.

And the strangest thing of all was how the two worlds bordered each other, how close together they were! For example, when our maid Lina sat by the parlor door at our evening prayers and joined in the hymn with her bright voice, her scrubbed hands flat on her smoothed-down apron, she belonged totally with Father and Mother, with us, with brightness and correctness. Immediately afterward, in the kitchen or woodshed, when she told me the story of the headless gnome or wrangled with female neighbors in the little butcher shop, she was someone else, she belonged to the other world, she was enveloped in mystery. And so it was with everything, especially with myself. Naturally, I belonged to the bright and correct world, I was my parents' child; but wherever I turned my eyes and ears, the other world was there and I lived in it, too, even though it was often unfamiliar and uncanny to me, even though I regularly got pangs of conscience and anxiety from it. In fact, at times I preferred to live in the forbidden world, and frequently my return home to the bright realm, no matter how necessary and good that might be, was almost like a return to someplace less beautiful, more boring and dreary. At times I knew my goal in life was to become like my father and mother, just as bright and pure, superior and well-ordered as they. But that was a long road to travel; before you got there, you had to attend schools and study and take tests and exams, and the road constantly led you alongside that other, darker world, and right through it, so that it was quite possible to get stuck there and go under. There were stories of prodigal sons to whom that had happened; I had read them excitedly. Their return home to their father and a good life was always so satisfying and splendid; I realized keenly that that was the only proper, good, and desirable outcome, but the part of the story that took place among the wicked and the lost was by far the more appealing, and, if one was free to state and admit it, it was sometimes actually a downright shame that the prodigal repented and was found again. But one didn't say that and didn't even think about it. The idea was merely somehow present as a premonition or possibility, deep down in your mind. When I visualized the Devil, I could quite easily imagine him down in the street, disguised or clearly identifiable, or else at the fair, or in a tavern, but never in our house.

My sisters also belonged to the bright world. It often seemed to me that their nature was closer to our father's and mother's; they were better, more well-behaved, faultless compared to me. They had shortcomings, they could be naughty, but, as I saw it, that wasn't very serious, it wasn't as it was with me; in my case, contact with evil was often so burdensome and torturing, the dark world was much nearer at hand. Like my parents, my sisters were people to be protected and honored; after any fight with them, my own conscience declared me to be the one in the wrong, the instigator, the one who had to ask forgiveness. For, by insulting my sisters, I was insulting my parents, the good and imposing faction. There were secrets I could much sooner share with the coarsest street boys than with my sisters. On good days, days of brightness and an untroubled conscience, it was often delightful to play with my sisters, to be good to them and well-behaved, and to see myself in a fine and noble aura. That's how it must be to be an angel! That was the highest goal within our ken, and we imagined it was sweet and wonderful to be an angel, enveloped in bright music and fragrance, like Christmas and happiness. Oh, how seldom it was possible to live such hours and days! Often while playing, playing good, inoffensive, permissible games, I became too excited and violent for my sisters to put up with; this led to arguments and unhappiness, and when anger overcame me at such times, I was a terror, doing and saying things whose vileness I felt deeply and painfully at the very moment I did and said them. Then came vexing, dark hours of regret and contrition, and then the awful moment when I asked to be forgiven, and then once again a ray of brightness, a silent, grateful sense of undivided happiness that would last hours or only moments.

I attended grammar school; the mayor's son and the son of the chief forest ranger were in my class and visited me sometimes; though wild boys, they nevertheless belonged to the good, permissible world. And yet I had close relations with neighbor boys who went to the ordinary elementary school, boys we usually looked down on. It's with one of them that I must begin my story.

On one afternoon when there were no classes—I was not much more than ten years old—I was hanging around with two boys from the neighborhood. Then a bigger boy joined us, a burly, rough fellow of about thirteen, from the elementary school, the son of a tailor. His father drank and his whole family had a bad reputation. I knew Franz Kromer well and I was afraid of him, so I didn't like him joining us then. He already acted like a grown-up man, mimicking the walk and speech habits of the young factory laborers. With him as the leader, we went down to the riverbank next to the bridge and hid from the world under the first arch of the bridge. The narrow bank between the vaulted bridge wall and the sluggishly flowing water consisted entirely of refuse, broken crockery and junk, tangled clusters of rusty wire and other rubbish. Sometimes usable items could be found there; under Franz Kromer's direction, we had to examine the stretch of ground and show him what we discovered. Then he either pocketed it or threw it into the water. He ordered us to pay special attention to any lead, brass, or pewter items that might be there; he pocketed them all, as well as an old horn comb. I felt very tense in his presence, not because I knew my father would forbid me to associate with him if he knew about it, but out of fear of

Franz himself. I was glad that he took me along and treated me like the others. He gave orders and we obeyed, as if it was an old custom, even though I was with him for the first time.

Finally, we sat down on the ground; Franz spat into the water and looked like a grown man. He spat through a gap in his teeth and could hit any mark he aimed at. A conversation began, and the boys started boasting and showing off, relating all sorts of schoolboy heroics and mischievous pranks. I kept silent but was afraid that this very silence would draw attention to me and make Kromer angry at me. From the outset my two companions had withdrawn from me and gone over to his side; I was a stranger among them, and I felt that my clothing and manners provoked them. As a grammar-school pupil and a "rich kid," I couldn't possibly be popular with Franz, and I was well aware that, the minute it came to that, the other two would disavow me and leave me in the lurch.

At last, out of pure fear, I started telling a story, too. I made up an elaborate tale of thievery, making myself the hero. My story was that, in an orchard near the Corner Mill, along with a friend I had stolen a sackful of apples at night, and not just ordinary apples but exclusively Reinettes and Golden Pearmains, the best varieties. I took refuge in this story from the dangers of the moment; I was a fluent inventor and teller of tales. In order not to finish too soon and thus perhaps become involved in something worse, I showed off all my inventive skills. One of us, I narrated, had to stand guard the whole time that the other one was in the tree throwing down the apples; and the sack was so heavy that we finally had to open it again and leave half the apples behind, but we returned a half-hour later and fetched the rest.

When I was finished, I hoped for a little applause; I had gradually become enthusiastic and intoxicated by my own yarn-spinning.

The two younger boys were silent in expectation, but Franz Kromer looked at me penetratingly through half-closed eyes and asked me in a menacing voice: "Is that true?"

"Yes," I said.

"So it's really and truly so?"

"Yes, really and truly," I definitely affirmed while choking inwardly with anxiety.

"Can you swear to it?"

I got very frightened, but I immediately said yes.

"Then say: 'By God and my salvation!'"

I said: "By God and my salvation."

"All right, then," he said, and he turned away.

I thought that was the end of it, and I was glad when shortly afterward he stood up and started walking back. When we were on the bridge, I immediately said that I had to go home.

"Don't be in such a hurry," Franz laughed, "after all, we're going the same way."

He sauntered ahead slowly, and I didn't dare to take a break for it, but he did actually walk towards our house. When we were there, when I saw our house door with its thick brass knob, the sunshine in the windows and the curtains in my mother's room, I drew a deep breath of relief. Oh, I was back home! Oh, I had made a good, blessed return home, a return to brightness and peace!

When I opened the door quickly and slipped inside, prepared to close it behind me, Franz Kromer pushed his way in, too. He stood beside me in the cool, dark passage with its tiled floor, where the light came only from the yard; he held me by the arm and said quietly: "Hey, you, don't rush away like that!"

I looked at him in fright. His grip on my arm was as hard as iron. I thought about his possible intentions and whether he might want to hit me. If I were to call out now, I thought, call out loudly and violently, would someone from upstairs show up fast enough to rescue me? But I decided not to.

"What is it?" I asked. "What do you want?"

"Not much. I just have to ask you something else. The others don't need to hear it."

"Is that right? Well, what else am I supposed to tell you? I've got to go upstairs, you know."

Franz said quietly, "I'm sure you know who owns the orchard by the Corner Mill."

"No, I don't. I think the miller."

Franz had flung his arm around me and now he drew me very close to himself, so that I was forced to look directly into his face. His eyes were malicious, he had a nasty smile, and his face was full of cruelty and power.

"Yes, boy, I'm the one who can tell you who owns the orchard. I've known for some time that the apples were stolen, and I also know that the man said he'd give two marks to whoever could tell him who stole the fruit."

"My God!" I exclaimed. "But you won't tell him anything, will you?"

I felt that it would be useless to appeal to his sense of honor. He came from that other world, for him backstabbing was no crime. I was completely convinced of that. In matters like this, the people from the "other" world weren't like us.

"Not tell him anything?" Kromer laughed. "My dear friend, do you think I'm a counterfeiter and can make my own two-mark pieces? I'm a poor guy, I don't have a rich father like you, and whenever I can earn two marks, I've got to earn them. Maybe he'll even give more."

He suddenly let go of me again. Our vestibule no longer smelt of peace and security; the world was tumbling down around me. He was going to turn me in, I was a criminal, my father would be informed, maybe the police would actually come. All the terrors of chaos threatened me, everything ugly and dangerous was mustered up against me. That I hadn't really stolen anything was completely beside the point. On top of that, I had sworn an oath. My God, my God!

Tears welled up in my eyes. I felt that I had to buy myself off, and I rummaged desperately through all my pockets. There was nothing in them, not an apple, not a pocket knife. Then I remembered my watch. It was an old silver watch, and it didn't go; I wore it "just for the sake of it." It came from our grandmother. I quickly pulled it out.

"Kromer," I said, "listen, you mustn't turn me in, that wouldn't be nice of you. I'll give you my watch, look; unfortunately, I have nothing else. You can have it, it's silver, and the work is good; it just has a minor defect, it has to be repaired."

He smiled and took the watch into his large hand. I looked at that hand and felt how rough and deeply hostile it was to me, how it was reaching out for my life and my peace of mind.

"It's silver," I said timidly.

"I don't give a hoot for your silver or that old watch of yours!" he said with profound contempt. "Get it repaired yourself!"

"But, Franz," I exclaimed, trembling with the fear that he might run away. "Please wait a minute! Do take the watch! It's real silver, really and truly. And I just don't have anything else."

He looked at me with cool contempt.

"In that case, you know who I'm going to see. Or I can also tell the police about it; I'm well acquainted with the sergeant."

He turned around to leave. I held him back by the sleeve. It mustn't be! I would much rather have died than bear all that would ensue if he left like that.

"Franz," I pleaded, hoarse with agitation, "don't do anything silly! It's just a joke, right?"

"Yes, a joke, but one that can cost you dear."

"Then, Franz, tell me what I should do! You know I'll do anything!"

He surveyed me with his half-shut eyes and laughed again.

"Don't be stupid!" he said with false bonhomie. "You know what's just the same as I do. I can earn two marks, and I'm not so rich that I can throw them away, you know it. But you're rich, you even have a watch. All you need to do is give me the two marks, and that will be that."

I understood his logic. But two marks! For me, it was as much, and just as impossible to get, as ten, a hundred, a thousand marks. I had no money. There was a little money-savings box in my mother's room that contained a few ten-pfennig and five-pfennig coins from uncles' visits and similar occasions. Otherwise, I had nothing. At that age, I wasn't yet receiving any allowance.

"I have nothing," I said sadly. "I have no money at all. But, aside from that, I'll give you anything. I have a book about Indians, soldiers, and a compass. I'll get it for you."

Kromer merely twitched his brazen, malicious lips and spat on the floor.

"Don't babble!" he said imperiously. "You can keep your junk. A compass! Don't make me angry now, too, alright? And hand over the money!"

"But I don't have any, I never get money. I just can't help it!"

"Well, then, you'll bring me the two marks tomorrow. After school, I'll be waiting down in the Market. And that's that. If you don't bring money, you'll see!"

"Yes, but where am I to get it from, when I haven't got any?"

"You've got enough money in the house. That's your affair. So then, tomorrow after school. And I'm telling you: if you don't bring it—" He darted a frightening look into my eyes, spat again, and disappeared like a ghost.

I was unable to go upstairs. My life was wrecked. I thought about running away and never coming back, or drowning myself. But I had no clear images of that. In the darkness, I sat down on the lowest step of the staircase, withdrew deeply into myself, and surrendered myself to my misfortune. Lina found me crying there when she came downstairs with a basket to fetch wood.

I asked her not to say anything upstairs, and I went up. On the rack beside the glass door hung my father's hat and my mother's parasol; domesticity and tenderness radiated to me from all those objects, my heart greeted them beseechingly and gratefully, just as the prodigal son greeted the sight and smell of the old rooms in his home. But now all of that was no longer mine, it was all part of the bright world of my father and mother, and I had sunk, guilt-laden, deep into the strange waters, entangled in intrigue and sin, threatened by my enemy and a prey to perils, anxiety, and shame. The hat and parasol, the good old freestone floor, the big picture over the vestibule closet, and the voice of my older sister coming from the parlor, all that was dearer, more gentle and precious than ever, but it no longer spelled consolation and solid possession, it was nothing but reproach. All that was no longer mine, I couldn't participate in its serenity and tranquillity. There was dirt on my shoes that I couldn't scrape off on the mat;

I carried shadows along with me that were unknown to the world of my home. I had had plenty of secrets in the past, and plenty of anxiety, but that was all a game and a joke in comparison with what I was carrying with me into these rooms today. Fate was hounding me, hands were reaching out at me from which my mother couldn't protect me, of which she shouldn't even learn. Whether my crime was a theft or lie (hadn't I sworn a false oath by God and my salvation?) didn't matter. My sin wasn't any particular action, my sin was having given my hand to the Devil. Why had I gone along? Why had I obeyed Kromer, more readily than I had ever obeyed my father? Why had I concocted that story about stealing? Why had I boasted about crimes as though they were heroic deeds? Now the Devil had me by the hand, now my enemy was after me.

For a moment, what I felt was no longer fear about the next day, but above all the terrible certainty that my path now led farther and farther downhill and into darkness. I perceived distinctly that my transgression must necessarily be followed by new transgressions, that rejoining my sisters, greeting and kissing my parents, was a lie, that I was carrying a destiny and secret with me that I was concealing within me.

For a moment, trust and hope blazed up in me, when I contemplated my father's hat. I would tell him everything, I would accept his sentence and his punishment and make him my confidant and rescuer. It would only be a penance of the sort I had often undergone, a difficult, bitter hour, a difficult and repentant request for forgiveness.

What a sweet sound that had! How appealing and tempting it was! But nothing came of it. I knew I wouldn't do it. I knew that now I had a secret, a guilt that I had to swallow on my own, all by myself. Perhaps I was at the crossroads right now, perhaps from this time on I would belong to the bad element forever and ever, sharing secrets with evil people, depending on them, obeying them, necessarily becoming like them. I had played the role of a grown man, of a hero; now I had to endure the consequences.

I was glad that, when I walked in, my father dwelt on my wet shoes. It was a diversion, he didn't notice what was worse, and I was allowed to undergo a reproach which I secretly applied to all the rest. As that happened, a strangely novel feeling was aroused in me, a malicious corrosive feeling full of barbs: I felt superior to my father! For the time of a moment, I felt a certain contempt for his ignorance, his scolding on account of my wet shoes seemed petty to me. "If you only knew!" I thought, and I felt like a criminal being interrogated about a stolen bread roll whereas he could have confessed to murders. It was an ugly, repellent feeling, but it was strong and had a profound attractiveness; more than any other notion, it chained me more tightly to my secret and my guilt. Perhaps, I thought, Kromer has already gone to the police and turned me in, and storm clouds are gathering over me while I'm being treated here like a little child!

Out of that whole experience, to the extent that I have narrated it up to here, that moment was the important and lasting element. It was the first rift in my father's sanctity, it was the first nick in the pillars on which my childish life had rested, and which every human being must destroy before he can become himself. It is of these experiences, invisible to everyone, that the inner, essential line of our destiny consists. That kind of rift and Nick closes over again, it is healed and forgotten, but in the most secret chamber of the mind it continues to live and bleed.

I was immediately terrified by this new feeling; I could have kissed my father's feet right away, in order to apologize to him for it. But nothing so fundamental can be apologized for, and a child feels and knows that, just as well and profoundly as any wise man does.

I felt the need to think over my situation, to make plans for the following day, but I didn't get that far. I was occupied that entire evening solely by getting used to the altered atmosphere in our parlor. It was as if the wall clock and the table, the Bible and the mirror, the bookshelf and the pictures on the wall were saying good-bye to me; with a heart growing cold I had to watch my world, my good, happy life, becoming the past and detaching itself from me; I had to perceive that I was anchored and held fast outside in the unfamiliar darkness by thirsty new roots. For the first time I tasted death, and death tastes bitter because it is birth, it is anxiety and terror in the face of a frightening innovation.

I was happy when I was finally lying in my bed! Before that, as my final purgatory, I had had to endure our evening prayers, during which we had sung a hymn that was one of my favorites. Oh, I didn't join in, and every note was gall and wormwood to me. I didn't join the prayer when my father spoke the blessing, and when he ended "...upon us all!" I was convulsively torn out of their circle. The grace of God was upon them all, but no longer upon me. I left, cold and enormously weary.

In bed, after lying there a while, lovingly enveloped in warmth and security, my heart in its fear wandered back again, fluttering anxiously over what had occurred. As always, my mother had said good night to me; her steps still echoed in the room, the glow of her candle still shone through the opening in the door. Now, I thought, now she'll come back again—she's felt what's going on—she'll give me a kiss and she'll ask me about it, ask me kindly and promisingly, and then I'll be able to cry, then the stone in my throat will melt, then I'll throw my arms around her and tell her everything, then things will be alright, then I'll be saved! And when the door opening had already grown dark, I still listened a while and thought that it just had to happen.

Then I returned to reality and looked my enemy in the eye. I saw him clearly, he had half-shut one eye, his mouth was laughing coarsely, and while I looked at him and bitterly acknowledged the inevitable, he became bigger and uglier, and his malicious eyes flashed devilishly. He was right beside me until I fell asleep, but then I didn't dream about him or that day's events; instead, I dreamt we were sailing in a boat, my parents and sisters and I, surrounded by the perfect peace and glow of a holiday. In the middle of the night I awoke, still feeling the aftertaste of bliss, still seeing my sisters' white summer dresses shimmering in the sunlight, and I relapsed from all that paradise into the reality of my situation; once more I was confronting my enemy with his malicious eyes.

In the morning, when my mother arrived hastily, calling out that it was already late and asking why I was still in bed, I looked sick; when she asked if anything was wrong with me, I vomited.

That seemed like a small gain to me. I very much liked being slightly ill and being able to stay in bed all morning with chamomile tea, listening to my mother tidying up in the next room, and to Lina greeting the butcher out in the vestibule. A morning without school was something enchanted, like a fairy tale; the sun would poke around in the room, and it wasn't the same sun that we shut out in school by lowering the green curtains. But even that had no savor today; it had taken on a false note.

Yes, if only I had died! But I was merely a little unwell, as often in the past, and nothing was accomplished thereby. It protected me from school, but it in no way protected me from Kromer, who would be waiting for me in the Market around eleven.

And this time my mother's friendliness offered no comfort; it was burdensome, and it hurt. Soon I pretended to be asleep again, and I thought things were over. There was no help for it, I had to be in the Market at eleven. And so I got up quietly at ten and said that I felt well again. As usual in such instances, it meant that I either had to go back to bed or attend school in the afternoon. I said I'd like to go to school. I had devised a plan.

I couldn't meet Kromer without money. I had to get my hands on the little money box that belonged to me. There wasn't enough money in it, I was well aware, not nearly enough; but it was still something, and a premonition told me that something was better than nothing, and that Kromer had to be at least pacified.

I was in low spirits when I crept into my mother's room in my stocking feet and took my box out of her desk, but it wasn't as bad as the events of the previous day. The pounding of my heart choked me, and it didn't get better when, down in the stairwell, I discovered on my first investigation that the box was locked. It was very easy to break it open; I merely had to rip apart a thin tin grating; but it hurt me to rip it open, because it was only then that I had committed a theft. Up until then, I had merely filched some tidbit, sugar lumps or fruit. But this was stealing, even if it was my own money. I felt that I had taken one more step nearer to Kromer and his world, that bit by bit I was fairly headed downhill, and I retorted by defiance. Let the Devil carry me away, now there was no turning back! I counted the money fearfully; while it was in the box it had sounded like such a lot, but now in my hand there was miserably little of it. It came to sixty-five pfennigs. I hid the box in the vestibule, held the money in my clenched fist, and left the house, feeling different from any other time I had walked through that gate. From upstairs someone called after me, it seemed; I departed swiftly.

There was still plenty of time; I sneaked by round-about paths through the narrow streets of a changed town, beneath clouds never seen before, past houses that looked at me and people who were suspicious of me. On the way, I recalled that one of my school chums had once found a thaler coin in the Cattle Market. I would gladly have prayed to God to perform a miracle and let me make such a find, too. But I no longer had any right to pray. And, even so, the money box wouldn't have been made whole again.

Franz Kromer saw me from a distance, but he walked toward me very slowly, seeming to pay no attention to me. When he was close to me, he signaled to me imperiously to follow him, and continued walking calmly, without looking around even once, down Straw Lane and over the footbridge until halting among the last houses, in front of a construction site. No work was going on there, the walls stood there bare without doors or windows. Kromer looked around and went in through the doorway, and I followed. He stepped behind the wall, beckoned me over, and held out his hand.

"Have you got it?" he asked coolly.

I drew my clenched fist out of my pocket and shook out my money onto the palm of his hand. He had counted it even before the last five-penning piece stopped clicking.

"This is sixty-five pennies," he said, and he looked at me.

"Yes," I said timidly. "That's all I have, I know it's not enough. But that's all there is. I have no more."

"I had thought you were smarter," he said, scolding me almost gently. "Between men of honor things should be orderly. I don't want to take anything from you unjustly, you know that.

Take back your small change! That other man—you know who—won't try to beat down my price. He'll pay."

"But I simply don't have any more! This came from my money box."

"That's your affair. But I don't want to drive you to despair. You still owe me one mark and thirty-five pennies. When will I get it?"

"Oh, you'll definitely get it, Kromer! I don't know right now—maybe I'll have more soon, tomorrow or the day after. You realize I can't talk to my father about it."

"That doesn't concern me. I'm not the type to do you harm. After all, I could get my money before noon, see? And I'm poor. You're wearing nice clothes, and you get better stuff to eat for lunch than I do. But I say no more. For my part, I can wait a while. Day after tomorrow I'll whistle for you, in the afternoon, then you'll settle up. Do you know my whistle?"

He performed it for me. I had heard it often.

"Yes," I said, "I know."

He went away as if I had nothing to do with him. It had been a business transaction between us, nothing more.

Even today, I think, Kromer's whistle would give me a start if I heard it again suddenly. From that time on I heard it frequently; I seemed to be hearing it constantly. There was no place, no game, no task, no thought that that whistle didn't pierce through; it robbed me of my independence, it was now my fate. I spent a lot of time in our little flower garden, which I loved, during the gentle, colorful autumn afternoons; and a peculiar urge led me to play childish games of earlier years once more; to some extent, I was playing the role of a boy younger than I actually was, a boy still good and free, innocent and secure. But in the midst of it, always unexpected and yet always frightfully disruptive and surprising,

Kromer's whistle came from somewhere or other, cutting the thread, destroying the illusions. Then I had to go, had to follow my tormentor to bad, ugly places, had to make an accounting to him and be dunned for money. The whole thing lasted a few weeks, perhaps, but it felt to me like years or eternity. I seldom had money, a five—or ten-pfennig coin stolen from the kitchen table when Lina left her shopping basket lying there. Each time, Kromer bawled me out and heaped scorn on me; I was the one who wanted to fool him and cheat him out of what was duly his; I was the one who was stealing from him; I was the one who was making him miserable! Not often in my life have I taken my distress so much to heart, never have I experienced greater hopelessness or loss of independence.

I had filled the money box with game tokens and put it back where it was; no one asked about it. But that, too, could come down around my ears any day. Even more than Kromer's vulgar whistle, I often feared my mother when she walked up to me softly—wasn't she coming to ask me about the money box?

Since I had presented myself to my devil without money several times, he began to torture and exploit me in another way. I had to work for him. He had to make deliveries for his father, and I had to make them for him. Or else he commanded me to perform some difficult feat, to hop on one leg for ten minutes or to attach a scrap of paper to a passerby's coat. Many nights in dreams I continued suffering these torments and lay bathed in sweat from those nightmares.

For a while I became ill. I vomited frequently and was subject to chills, though at night I was sweaty and feverish. My mother felt that something was wrong, and displayed a lot of sympathy, which tortured me because I couldn't respond to her confidence.

One evening when I was already in bed she brought me a piece of chocolate. That was a reminiscence of earlier years in which on many evenings, when I had been well-behaved, I had received similar comforting tidbits at bedtime. Now she stood there and held out the piece of chocolate to me. I felt so bad that all I could do was shake my head. She asked what was wrong with me, and stroked my hair. I could merely blurt out: "No! No! I don't want anything." She put the chocolate on the night table and left. When she tried to ask me about it the following day, I pretended I didn't remember anything about it. Once she sent for the doctor to see me; he examined me and left instructions that I should wash in cold water every morning.

My condition in that period was a sort of insanity. In the midst of our household's orderly, peaceful existence I was living as frightened and tormented as a ghost; I didn't participate in the life of the others, and rarely took my mind off my troubles even for an hour. With my father, who was often irritated and questioned me, I was cold and reserved.

CHAPTER 2

CAIN

Rescue from my tortures came from an altogether unexpected quarter, and along with it something new came into my life, something that has affected it to this very day.

Shortly before this time, a new pupil had been enrolled in our grammar school. He was the son of a well-to-do widow who had moved to our town, and he wore a crepe band on his sleeve. He was in a higher grade than I was, and he was several years older, but he soon caught my attention, as he did everybody's. This remarkable pupil seemed to be much older than he looked; no one got the impression that he was just a boy. In the midst of our childish crowd, he moved about like a stranger, as mature as a man or, rather, a gentleman. He wasn't popular, he didn't take part in our games, let alone our fights; the only thing about him the rest of us liked was the self-confident, firm tone in which he addressed the teachers. His name was Max Demian.

It happened one day, as it did occasionally in our school, that for some reason or other a second class was placed in our very large classroom. It was Demian's class. The younger ones had Bible History, the older ones had to write an essay. While the story of Cain and Abel was being hammered into us, I glanced over at Demian many times (his face had a strange fascination for me), and I saw that clever, bright, unusually mature face bent over his work attentively and intelligently. He didn't look at all like a schoolboy doing an assignment, but like a scholar pursuing his own research. I didn't find him pleasant, to tell the truth; on the contrary, I had something against him; he was too superior and cool to suit me, I found him too provokingly self-confident by nature, and his eyes had that grown-up expression that children never like, a little sad, with flashes of mockery in it. And yet I had to look at him again and again, whether I liked him or not; but when he glanced at me once, I immediately looked away in fright. When I think today about his appearance then as a schoolboy, I can say: in every respect, he was different from the rest; he was thoroughly original and individual, and attracted attention that way—yet, at the same time, he did all he could not to attract attention; he bore and behaved himself like a prince in disguise in the midst of farmboys, making every effort to resemble them.

On the way home from school he walked behind me. After the others had scattered, he caught up with me and said hello. His greeting, too, even though he was imitating our schoolboy manner, was just as grown-up and courteous.

"Can we walk a way together?" he asked amicably. I was flattered and I nodded yes. Then I described my house to him.

"Oh, there?" he said with a smile. "I already know that house. Over your door there's a peculiar thing fixed to the wall; it interested me right off."

At first, I didn't know what he meant, and I was amazed that he seemed to know our house better than I did. Yes, as a keystone over the entrance arch there was a kind of coat-of-arms, but over time it had been worn away and had frequently been painted over; as far as I knew, it had nothing to do with us or our family.

"I don't know anything about it," I said timidly. "It's a bird or something of the sort; it must be very old. They say the house was once part of the monastery."

"That may well be," he nodded. "Just take a good look at it! Things like that are often interesting. I think it's a sparrowhawk."

We kept walking; I was quite intrigued. Suddenly Demian laughed as if something had struck him as funny.

"Yes, I was there during your lesson," he said animatedly. "The story of Cain, who had a mark on his forehead, right? Do you like it?"

No, I had rarely liked any part of all the stuff we had to learn. But I didn't dare say so; it was as if an adult were talking with me. I said I liked the story line.

Demian tapped me on the shoulder.

"You don't have to pretend with me, friend. But the story is actually very peculiar; I think it's much more peculiar than most others that occur in the course. In fact, the teacher didn't say much about it, merely the usual remarks about God, sin, and so forth. But I think." He broke off, smiled, and asked: "But does this interest you?"

"Well, then," he resumed, "I think this story of Cain can be understood in a completely different way. Most of the things we're taught are certainly quite true and correct, but they can also all be viewed in a way different from the teachers', and then they generally make much better sense. For instance, it's very hard to be satisfied with this Cain and the mark on his forehead the way it's explained to us. Don't you think so, too? That someone kills his brother during an argument, yes, that can certainly happen, and that he gets scared afterward and climbs down a peg, that's possible, too. But that he is especially rewarded for his cowardice with a medal of distinction that protects him and frightens everyone else, is really odd, you must admit."

"Of course," I said, showing interest; the subject was beginning to entrance me. "But how can you explain the story differently?"

He tapped my shoulder.

"Very simply! What actually existed and gave rise to the story in the first place was the mark. There was a man with something on his face that frightened others. They didn't dare touch him; he made an impression on them, he and his children. Maybe, or certainly, there wasn't really a mark on his forehead, like a postmark; in real life, things are rarely that crude. Surely it was something strange that was barely noticeable, a little more intelligence and daring in his eyes than people were used to. This man had power, people shied away from this man. He had a 'mark.' They explained it any way they wanted. And 'they' always want what's convenient for them and puts them in the right. They were afraid of the children of Cain, who possessed a 'mark.' And so they explained the mark not for what it was, as a distinction, but as the opposite. They said that fellows with that mark were weird, and so they were. People with courage and character always seem weird to other people. It was very uncomfortable to have a race of fearless, weird people running around, so now they hung a nickname on that race and made up a story about it in order to take revenge on it, in order to be compensated to some extent for all the fear they had undergone. – Understand?"

"Yes—that is—in that case, Cain wasn't evil at all? And the whole story in the Bible is actually completely untrue?"

"Yes and no. Stories that are so old, so very ancient, are always true, but they aren't always correctly noted down and explained.

In short, I think Cain was a terrific guy, and people made up that story about him just because they were afraid of him. The story was simply a rumor, something that people bandied around in their gossip; it was true to the extent that Cain and his children really bore a kind of 'mark' and were different from most people."

I was completely amazed.

"And so you think the part about the murder isn't true, either?" I asked about my consuming interest.

"Oh, yes! It's certainly true. The strong man killed a weak man. Whether it was really his brother may be doubted. It's unimportant; when you come down to it, all men are brothers. And so a strong man murdered a weak man. Maybe it was a heroic deed, maybe not. But in any case the other weak men were now terror-stricken, they lamented loudly, and when they were asked, 'Why don't you just kill him, too?' they didn't say, 'Because we're cowards,' they said, 'We can't. He's got a mark. God has set a mark on him!' The hoax must have started in some such way. Oh, I'm holding you up. So long!"

He turned into Old Street and left me alone, more puzzled than I had ever been. The moment he was gone, I found everything he had said totally unbelievable! Cain a noble person, Abel a coward! The mark of Cain is a distinction! It was absurd, it was blasphemous and wicked. Where was God in all of this? Hadn't He accepted Abel's sacrifice, didn't He love Abel? No, this was nonsense! And I supposed that Demian had been pulling my leg and sending me up the garden path. To be sure, he was a damned clever fellow, and he could talk, but all this—no.

And yet I had never before thought so much about any story from the Bible or elsewhere. And for a long time, I hadn't forgotten Franz Kromer so completely, hours at a time, for a whole evening. At home I read through the story again as it stood in the Bible; it was short and clear, and to look for some special, secret interpretation was totally crazy. Then any murderer could claim to be God's favorite! No, that was nonsense. The only good thing about it was the way that Demian could come out with such a theory, so readily and neatly, as if it were all self-evident, and with that look in his eyes, to boot!

In truth, my own existence wasn't totally in order; in fact, it was in great disarray. I had lived in a bright, clean world, I had been a sort of Abel, and now I was so deep in the 'other' element, I had fallen and sunk so low, and yet basically I couldn't do much to help myself! How did things stand in that quarter? Yes, now a memory flashed through my head that almost took my breath away for a minute. On that terrible evening when my present misery had begun, that incident with my father had taken place; for the space of a moment, I had suddenly seemed to see through, and to despise him and his bright world and wisdom! Yes, then I, in the role of Cain and bearing his mark, had imagined that that mark was no shame, but a distinction, and that through my malice and wretchedness I ranked above my father, above good and pious men.

At the time I didn't experience the matter with such clarity of thought, but all these elements were included in it; it was a simple flaring up of emotions, of strange stirrings that gave me pain and yet filled me with pride.

When I thought things over—how oddly Demian had spoken about the fearless and the cowardly! How strangely he had interpreted the mark on Cain's forehead! And, as he did so, how peculiarly his remarkable eyes had glistened, those grown-up eyes! And it darted vaguely through my head: this Demian, isn't he a sort of Cain? Why does he defend him if he doesn't feel similar to him? Why does he have that power in this gaze? Why does he speak so scornfully about "the others," the timorous people, who after all are the pious, those in whom God takes pleasure?

I couldn't think these thoughts through to any conclusion. A stone had fallen into the well, and the well was my young soul. And for a long, a very long time, this matter of Cain, the murder, and the mark was the point of origin of all my attempts at gaining knowledge, formulating doubts, and examining things critically.

I noticed that the other pupils were very preoccupied with Demian, too. I hadn't told anyone about the incident concerning Cain, but he seemed to interest others as well. At any rate, a lot of rumors about the "new boy" began to circulate. If I only still recalled all of them, they would shed some light on him, each of them could be interpreted. All I still recall is that the first bit of gossip was that Demian's mother was very rich. People also said that she never went to church, and not her son, either. Rumor had it they were Jews, or else they might be crypto-Muslims. Further tales were told about Max Demian's physical strength. What was certain was that, when the strongest boy in his class challenged him to a fight and called him a coward when he refused, Demian inflicted a stunning humiliation on him. Those who were present said that Demian had merely taken him by the neck with one hand and squeezed tight; then the boy turned pale, and afterward, he sneaked away and for days was unable to use his arm. For the space of an evening, people even said he had died. Everything was claimed for a while, everything was believed, everything was exciting and marvelous. Then people had enough for a time. But not long afterward new rumors arose among us schoolboys, some of whom felt free to report that Demian had intimate relations with girls and "knew all there was to know."

Meanwhile, my involvement with Franz Kromer pursued its inevitable course. I couldn't shake him off; even if he occasionally left me in peace for days at a time, I was still bound to him. He participated in my dreams like my shadow, and whatever harm he didn't do to me in reality, my imagination let him do in those dreams, in which I was his abject slave. I lived in those dreams—I was always a heavy dreamer—more than in real life; those shadows consumed my strength and life. Among other things, I frequently dreamt that Kromer was beating me, spitting on me, and kneeling on me, and, what was worse, that he lured me on to commit serious crimes—no, not so much lured me as simply forced me by means of his powerful influence; The most frightening of those dreams, from which I awoke half-crazy, included a murderous attack on my father. Kromer sharpened a knife and handed it to me; we were standing behind trees in a tree-lined avenue, lying in wait for someone, I didn't know whom; but when someone came by and Kromer indicated to me by pressure on my arm that that was the person I had to stab, it was my father. Then I awoke.

These things, of course, still made me think about Cain and Abel, but not so much about Demian anymore. When he first regained contact with me, it was also in a dream, strangely enough. It was like this: I dreamt again about being beaten and terrorized, but this time instead of Kromer it was Demian kneeling on me. And—this was entirely new and made a strong impression on me—all that Kromer had made me suffer in the way of torture and struggling against it, I accepted from Demian gladly and with an emotion made up just as much of pleasure as of fear. I had this dream twice, then Kromer returned to his original role.

What I experienced in these dreams and what was actually, I have been unable to distinguish clearly for some time now. In any case, my bad relationship with Kromer took its course, and was by no means finished when I had finally paid off the amount owed to him by a series of petty thefts. No, now he knew about those thefts, because he kept asking me where the money was coming from, and I was more in his power than ever before. He frequently threatened to tell my father everything, and then my anxiety was scarcely as strong as my deep regret at not having done so myself at the very outset. And yet, wretched as I felt, I still didn't regret everything, at least not at the time; at times I thought I felt things just had to be that way. I was under a cloud of calamity and it was pointless to try to break out of it.

Presumably, my parents suffered a great deal from this state of affairs. A strange spirit had come over me; I no longer belonged in our little community, which had been so intimate, and for which I was often assailed by an aching nostalgia, as if for lost Edens. I was treated, especially by my mother, more like a sick person than like a villain, but I could best discern the true state of things from the behavior of my two sisters toward me. This behavior, which was extremely considerate and yet made me infinitely miserable, indicated clearly that I was a sort of possessed person, whose condition was more to be pitied than blamed, but nevertheless one in whom evil had taken up residence. I was aware that I was being prayed for, not in the same way as in the past, and I felt how futile those prayers were. I often ardently perceived a longing for relief, the desire for a proper confession, but I also felt in advance that I would be unable to tell and explain things correctly to either my father or mother. I knew that they would receive my words amicably, they would carefully spare my feelings, in fact, pity me, but they wouldn't fully understand me, and the whole thing would be looked on as a sort of minor infraction, whereas it was actually my fate.

I know that many people won't believe that a child not yet eleven is capable of such feelings. It is not to those people that I am telling my story. I'm telling it to those who have greater knowledge of humanity. An adult who has learned how to transform part of his emotions into thought processes notices that such thoughts aren't present in a child, and then concludes that the experiences aren't present, either. But only seldom in my life have I had such deep and painful experiences as I had then.

One rainy day, when my tormentor had ordered me to meet him on Citadel Square, I was standing and waiting, burrowing with my toes in the wet chestnut leaves that still kept on falling from the black, dripping trees. I had no money, but I had stashed away two pieces of cake, which I was carrying with me so I could give Kromer something at least. I had long grown accustomed to standing around in a corner somewhere waiting for him, often for a very long time, and I accepted it passively, the way people accept what can't be changed.

Finally, Kromer arrived. That day he didn't stay long. He gave me a couple of pokes in the ribs, he laughed, he took my cake, and he even offered me a damp cigarette, which I didn't take; he was more friendly than usual.

"Yes," he said as he was leaving, "so I don't forget—next time you could bring along your sister, the older one. What's her name, anyway?"

I didn't understand, and I made no reply. I just looked at him in astonishment.

"Don't you get it? I want you to bring along your sister."

"I understand, Kromer, but I won't. I mustn't, and she wouldn't come, anyhow."

I expected that that was just another harassment and some kind of pretext. He did that frequently, making some impossible demands, frightening me, humiliating me, and then gradually arriving at some bargain. Then I would have to buy myself off with a little money or other gifts.

This time he was altogether different. He was scarcely angry at my refusal.

"All right," he said offhandedly, "think it over. I'd like to get acquainted with your sister. You'll see it's possible. All you need to do is take her along on one of your walks, and then I'll join you. Tomorrow I'll give you a whistle, then we'll talk about it again."

When he was gone, I suddenly had some inkling of what his request meant. I was still totally a child, but from gossip, I knew that when boys and girls were a little older, they were able to do some kind of secret, disgusting, and forbidden things with each other. And so now I was supposed to—all of a sudden it became clear to me how monstrous it was! At once I resolved firmly never to do it. But I hardly dared to think what would happen next and what sort of revenge Kromer would take on me. A new kind of torture was beginning for me, the rest hadn't been enough.

I walked across the empty square disconsolately, my hands in my pockets. New torments, new slavery!

Then a vigorous, deep voice called to me. I got frightened and started running. Someone was running after me, a hand grasped me gently from behind. It was Max Demian.

I surrendered.

"It's you?" I said unsteadily. "You gave me such a scare!"

He looked at me, and his gaze had never been more like that of an adult, a superior man of penetrating intelligence, than it now was. It was a long time since we had spoken to each other.

"I'm sorry," he said in his polite, but in a very resolute way. "But listen, no one should let himself get so scared."

"Well, it can happen."

"Apparently. But look: if you jump like that when someone comes along who has never harmed you, that someone starts to think about it. It surprises him, it makes him curious. That someone thinks to himself: it's strange how easily you get scared. And he goes on thinking: people only act that way when they have some anxiety. Cowards always feel anxiety, but I don't think you're really a coward, right? Oh, of course, you're no hero, either. There are things you're afraid of; there are also people you're afraid of. And there should never be any. No, no one should ever be afraid of people. You're not afraid of me, I hope? Or are you?"

"Oh, no, not at all."

"There, you see? But there are people you're afraid of?"

"I don't know... Leave me alone, what do you want of me?"

He was keeping pace with me—I had begun to walk faster, with the idea of running away—and I felt his gaze coming from one side.

"Just believe," he continued, "I wish you well. At any rate, you need to have some anxiety on my account. I'd like to experiment with you; it's entertaining and you can learn something very useful from it. Pay attention! Well, from time to time I attempt a trick called mind reading. There's no magic involved, but when you don't know how it's done, it looks very unusual. You can give people a big surprise with it. Now, let's try. You see, I like you, or I'm interested in you, and now I'd like to summon up your hidden thoughts. I've already taken the first step in that direction. I'm scared of you—and so you're easily scared. So there are things and people you're afraid of. Why should that be? No one needs to be afraid of anyone. If a person is afraid of someone, it's because he has allowed someone to acquire power over him. For example, he's done something wrong and the other person knows it—then he has power over you. Get it? It's surely clear, isn't it?"

I looked him in the face helplessly; his face was as serious and wise as always, and also kind, but without any sentimentality; it was severe, rather. It exhibited a sense of justice or something like that. I didn't know what was going on with me; he stood in front of me like a magician.

"Do you understand?" he asked again.

I nodded. I couldn't speak.

"As I said, mind-reading looks funny, but it's a quite natural process. For example, I could also tell you fairly accurately what you thought about me when I once explained the story of Cain and Abel to you. Well, this isn't the time to do so. I even think you may have dreamed about me. But let's drop that! You're a clever boy, most of them are so stupid! I enjoy talking from time to time with a clever boy whom I have confidence in. I hope it's alright with you?"

"Oh, yes. Only, I don't understand."

"Let's stick to the entertaining experiment! And so, we've found: Boy S— is easily frightened—he's afraid of somebody—he probably shares with that other person a secret that gives him great discomfort. Is that correct, more or less?"

As in a dream I was captivated by his voice, his influence. I merely nodded. Wasn't a voice speaking there that could only be issued from me? That knew everything? That knew everything better and more clearly than I did?

Demian gave me a hard tap on the shoulder.

"So it's correct. I thought as much. Now, just one more question: Do you know the name of the boy who walked away from here a while ago?"

I got terrifically frightened; my secret, now that it had been touched on, cringed painfully as it withdrew inside me, unwilling to face the light.

"What kind of boy? There was no boy here, just me."

He laughed.

"Speak up!" he laughed. "What's his name?"

I whispered: "Do you mean Franz Kromer?"

With an air of satisfaction, he nodded to me.

"Bravo! You're a smart fellow, we'll still be friends. But now I have to tell you something: This Kromer, or whatever his name is, is a bad fellow. His face tells me he's a scoundrel! What do you think?"

"Oh, yes," I sighed, "he's bad, he's a Satan! But he mustn't know any of this! For God's sake, he mustn't know a thing! Do you know him? Does he know you?"

"Please be calm. He's gone, and he doesn't know me—yet. But I'd very much like to make him acquainted. He attends the public elementary school?"

"Yes."

"In what grade?"

"The fifth. But say nothing to him! Please, please say nothing to him!"

"Be calm, nothing will happen to you. I suppose you don't feel like telling me a little more about this Kromer."

"I can't! No, leave me alone!"

He remained silent for a while.

"Too bad," he then said, "we could have continued the experiment further. But I don't want to torture you; But you do know—right? that your fear of him is something totally improper? A fear like that ruins us, we've got to get rid of it. You've got to get rid of it if you're to become a regular person. Do you understand?"

"Of course, you're perfectly right... but it's impossible. You just don't know..."

"You've seen that I know a lot, more than you would have thought. Do you owe him money, perhaps?"

"Yes, that also, but that isn't the main thing. I can't tell you, I can't!"

"So it wouldn't help if I gave you the amount you owe him? I could easily give it to you."

"No, no, it's not that. And I beg you: don't tell anyone about this! Not a word! You're driving me crazy."

"Rely on me, Sinclair. Sometime in the future, you'll tell me your secrets."

"Never, never," I shouted violently.

"Just as you wish. I only mean, maybe you'll tell me more sometime. Only if you're willing to, naturally! You surely don't think I'd behave the way Kromer does?"

"Oh, no—but, after all, you don't know anything about it!"

"Not a thing. I merely reflect on it. And I'll never behave the way Kromer behaves, I'm sure you believe that. Besides, you don't owe me anything."

We were silent for quite a while, and I grew calmer. But Demian's knowledge became more and more puzzling to me.

"I'm going home now," he said and drew his waterproof coat more tightly around him in the rain. "I'd just like to tell you one thing again, since we've come this far—you ought to get rid of that fellow! If it can't be done any other way, kill him! I'd be impressed and pleased if you did. I'd even help you."

I got frightened again. I suddenly recalled the story of Cain once more. The situation felt creepy, and I started to cry softly. There was too much weirdness in the air.

"All right, then," Max Demian smiled. "Get along home! We'll settle things yet. Though killing him would be the simplest thing. In such matters, the simplest method is always the best. It's no good for you to remain in your friend Kromer's hands."

I came home and felt as if I had been away for a year. Everything looked different. In my relations with Kromer, there was some hint of a future, of hope. I was no longer alone! And now I saw for the first time how terribly alone I had been with my secret for weeks and weeks. And the conclusion I had arrived at several times came to mind at once: that a confession to my parents would give me relief but wouldn't save me altogether, Now I had all but confessed, to someone else, to a stranger, and a premonition of redemption came to me like a heady fragrance!

Nevertheless, my anxiety was still far from overcoming, and I was still prepared for long, frightening confrontations with my enemy. I thus found it all the more peculiar that everything went by so quietly, in such complete secrecy and calm.

Kromer's whistle outside our house wasn't to be heard, for a day, two days, three days, a week. I didn't dare believe it, and remained mentally alert for his sudden reappearance just when least expected. But he was gone, and he stayed away! Not trusting this new freedom, I still didn't sincerely believe it. Until I once finally ran into Franz Kromer. He was walking down Ropemakers' Lane, right toward me. When he saw me he winced, puckered his face into an ugly grimace, and turned right around to avoid meeting me.

That was an extraordinary moment for me! My enemy was running away from me! My Satan was afraid of me! I was filled with joy and surprise.

Around that time Demian showed up again. He was waiting for me in front of the school.

"Hi!" I said.

"Good morning, Sinclair. I just wanted to find out how you're doing. Kromer is leaving you in peace now, isn't he?"

"Was that what you were doing? But how? How? I don't understand it. He doesn't show up at all anymore."

"Good. If he should ever come back—I don't think he will, but he is a fresh kid—then just tell him to think about Demian."

"But what's the connection? Did you pick a fight with him and beat him up?"

"No, I don't like to do that. I merely spoke to him, just as I did with you, and when I did, I was able to make it clear to him that it's to his own advantage to leave you in peace."

"Oh, you didn't give him any money, did you?"

"No, my friend. After all, you had already tested that method."

He tore himself away, no matter how hard I tried to ask him all the details, and I was left with that old uncomfortable feeling about him, that strange combination of gratitude and timidity, admiration and fear, affection and inner resistance.

I resolved to see him again soon, and talk to him some more about all that, and also about that business with Cain.

The meeting never took place.

Anyway, gratitude isn't a virtue I believe in, and to ask it of a child would seem like a mistake to me. And so I'm not very surprised at my own total ingratitude concerning Max Demian.

Today I firmly believe that I would have become ill and depraved for my whole life if he hadn't rescued me from Kromer's clutches. Even back then I already perceived that liberation as the greatest event in my young life—but I left the liberator himself on the sidelines the moment he had accomplished the miracle.

As I said, I don't find that ingratitude odd. The only thing I find peculiar is the lack of curiosity I displayed. How was it possible for me to go on living a single day in peace and quiet without delving into the mysteries that Demian had put me in contact with? How could I restrain the desire to hear more about Cain, more about Kromer, more about mind reading?

It's scarcely comprehensible, and yet it's so. I suddenly found myself disentangled from the demonic snares, I saw the world before me bright and joyous once more, I was no longer subject to anxiety attacks and heart palpitations that choked me. The spell was broken, I was no longer a lost soul in torment, I was once again a schoolboy as always. My mind and body sought to regain their equilibrium and calm as swiftly as possible, and so, above all, they made every effort to thrust away all that ugliness and menace, to forget it. With miraculous speed, the whole long story of my guilt and terrorization slipped out of my memory, apparently without leaving behind any scars or impressions.

Today it is equally understandable to me that I also tried to forget my helper and rescuer just as swiftly. I fled from the misery of my damnation, from my frightening enslavement to Kromer, with every urge and force of my injured soul; I fled back to where I had earlier been happy and contented: to the lost paradise that was opening up again, to the bright world of my father and mother, to my sisters, to the fragrance of purity, to Abel's desire to please God.

On the very day after my brief conversation with Demian, when I was finally completely convinced of my regained freedom and no longer feared any relapses, I did what I had so often and so ardently wished to do—I confessed. I went to my mother, I showed her the money box with its damaged lock, filled with game tokens instead of money, and I told her how long I had chained myself to a wicked torturer through my own fault. She didn't understand everything, but she saw the box, she saw the change in my expression, she heard the change in my voice, and she realized I had recovered and was restored to her.

And now with strong emotions, I celebrated the holiday of my restitution, the realm of the prodigal son. My mother took me to my father, the story repeated, questions and exclamations of astonishment followed one another rapidly, both my parents stroked my head and heaved a sigh of relief from that long-lasting oppressiveness. Everything was splendid, everything was like a storybook, everything was resolved into marvelous harmonies.

Now I took refuge in that harmony with genuine passion. I couldn't sate myself sufficiently with the thought that I had regained my peace of mind and my parents' trust; I became a homebody and a model boy; I played with my sisters more than ever before, and at prayers, I joined in the old hymns I loved with the emotions of one who has been saved and converted. It came from my heart, there was nothing false about it.

And yet things weren't in order! And this is the point that offers the only true explanation of the way I forgot about Demian. I should have made my confession to him! The confession would have been less decorative and touching, but it would have turned out more profitable for me. Now I was clinging with all my roots to my former heavenly world, I had returned home and had been restored to everyone's good graces. But Demian in no way belonged to that world, he didn't fit into it. He, too—not like Kromer, but nonetheless—he too was a seducer; he, too, tied me to that second, evil, bad world, and I no longer wanted to have anything to do with it. I couldn't and wouldn't sacrifice Abel and help to glorify Cain just when I had become an Abel again.

That was the external situation. But the mental one was this: I was free from Kromer's hands and the Devil's, but not thanks to my own strength and achievement. I had tried to walk the paths of the world and they had been too slippery for me. Now that the grasp of a friendly hand had saved me, I was running back, casting not another glance around me, to my mother's lap and the security of a sheltered, pious childhood. I made myself younger, more dependent, and more child-like than I was. I was compelled to exchange my dependency on Kromer for a new one, because I was unable to walk on my own. And so, in the blindness of my heart, I chose to be dependent on my father and mother, the beloved old "bright world," which I nevertheless already knew wasn't the only one. If I hadn't done that, I would have had to resort to Demian and entrust myself to him. At the time, my not doing so seemed to me to be a justifiable distrust of his disconcerting ideas; but in truth it was nothing but fear. Because Demian would have demanded more of me than my parents demanded, much more; by means of inducements and admonitions, sarcasm and irony, he would have tried to make me more self-reliant. Oh, I know it today: nothing in the world is more repugnant to a man than following the path that leads him to himself!

Nevertheless, about a half-year later, I couldn't resist the temptation and, on a walk with my father, I asked him what was to be thought of some people's declaration that Cain was better than Abel.

He was quite astonished and explained to me that this was far from a novel conception. It had even emerged in the Early Christian period, being taught by sects, one of which called itself "Cainites." But naturally, that insane doctrine was nothing but an attempt by the Devil to destroy our religion. Because if one believed that Cain was right and Abel was wrong, the consequence would be that God had made a mistake; in other words, that the God of the Bible wasn't the real and only one, but a false one. And in fact the Cainites had taught and preached something like that; but that heresy had long vanished from human ken, and his only cause for surprise was that a school chum of mine could have been able to hear anything about it. All the same, he said, he admonished me earnestly to abandon such thoughts.

CHAPTER 3

THE THIEF ON THE CROSS

I could tell lovely, tender, and lovable things about my childhood, about my secure existence with my father and mother, my childlike love for them, and my contentedly playful, dreamy existence in my gentle, loving, and bright surroundings. But I'm only interested in the steps I took in my life to arrive at myself. All the pretty periods of calm, islands of bliss, and Edens, whose magic I didn't fail to experience, I leave behind me in the glow of distance, and I have no desire to set foot on them again.

And so, for the rest of the time, I continue to dwell on my boyhood, I shall speak only about new things that happened to me, things that drove me onward or tore me away.

These impulses always came from the "other world," they were always accompanied by anxiety, compulsion, and a troubled conscience. They were always revolutionary, endangering the peace in which I would gladly have gone on living.

The years came in which I was once again forced to discover that a primordial urge dwelt within me myself, an urge that had to crawl away and hide from the bright, permissible world. As it happens to everyone, I too was attacked by the gradually awakening perception of sex as an enemy and destroyer, as something forbidden, as seduction and sin. What my curiosity sought, what caused me dreams, pleasure, and anxiety, the great mystery of puberty, just didn't fit into the sheltered happiness of my childlike peace. I did what everyone does. I led the double life of a child who really isn't a child anymore. My consciousness dwelt in the familiar, permissible world, my conscience denied the existence of the new world that was dawning. But at the same time, I was living in dreams, urges, and wishes of a subterranean kind, over which that conscious life built more and more anxious bridges, because my child's world was collapsing within me. Just like almost all parents, mine offered no help for my awakening life-urges, which weren't discussed. All they did—and this, with inexhaustible pains—was to aid me in my hopeless attempts to deny reality and keep on residing in a child's world that was becoming more and more unreal and falsified. I don't know whether parents can do much in these situations, and I'm casting no blame on mine. It was my own business to cope with myself and find my own path, and I conducted my business badly, just as most children do who have been well brought up.

Everyone lives through this difficult period. For the average person, it's the point in his life when the demands of his own life clash most violently with the world around him, when his forward path must be fought for most bitterly. Many experience this death and rebirth, which are our destiny, only this once in their life, when childhood decays and slowly disintegrates, when all that has become dear to us is about to leave us and we suddenly feel the solitude and deathly chill of outer space around us. And very many are hung up for good on this reef and for the rest of their life cling painfully to the irretrievable past, to the dream of the lost paradise, which is the worst and most murderous of all dreams.

Let's return to the story. The sensations and dream images in which the end of childhood was announced to me, aren't important enough to be narrated. The important thing was: the "dark world," the "other world" was back. What Franz Kromer had once represented was now within my own being. And therefore the "other world" regained its power over me externally as well.

Since that business with Kromer, several years have gone by. By then that dramatic, guilt-laden period of my life was very far from me, and seemed to have dissolved into nothingness like a brief nightmare. Franz Kromer had long since vanished from my life; I barely noticed it when I sometimes ran across him. But the other important figure in my tragedy, Max Demian, never again completely disappeared from my surroundings. And yet for a long time, he was far away and off to the side, visible but ineffectual. Only gradually did he approach again, once more radiating strength and influence.

I'm trying to recall what I know about Demian at that period. It's possible that for a year or more I didn't speak with him even once. I avoided him, and he never thrust himself upon me. Probably he nodded to me when we ran across each other. It then seemed to me at times as if his friendly greeting was tinged with a subtle hint of scorn or ironic reproach, but that might have been just my imagination. It was as if the events I had experienced with him, and the strange influence he had then exerted over me, were forgotten, both by him and by me.

I'm seeking his figure, and now that my thoughts turn back to him, I see that he was actually around and that I noticed him. I see him on his way to school, alone or with other older pupils, and I see him walking among them as a foreign body, solitary and silent, like a heavenly body surrounded by its own atmosphere, obeying its own laws. No one loved him, no one was close to him, except his mother, and even with her his behavior seemed not a child's, but an adult's. The teachers left him alone as much as they could—he was a good pupil—but he didn't try to please any of them, and from time to time we heard rumors of some remark, a touch of sarcasm or a retort, that he was supposed to have made to a teacher, a remark that was all that could be wished in the way of blunt provocation or irony.

I'm thinking back, my eyes closed, and I see his image arise. Where was that? Oh, yes, now I have it again. It was in the narrow street in front of our house. I saw him standing there one day holding a memo pad and drawing. He was drawing the old coat-of-arms with the bird that was over the door to our house. And I was standing at a window, hidden behind the curtain, watching him, and with profound astonishment, I saw his attentive, serene, bright face turned toward the coat-of-arms, the face of a grown man, a scholar or an artist, superior and full of willpower, unusually bright and serene, with knowing eyes.

And I see him again. It was not long afterward, in the street; on our way home from school, we were all standing around a horse that had fallen. It lay, still attached to the shafts, in front of a farm wagon, snuffling pitifully in the air with flaring nostrils as if searching for something, and bleeding from an unseen wound, so that on one side of it the white dust of the street was slowly growing dark as it absorbed the blood. When I turned away from that sight with a sensation of queasiness, I saw Demian's face. He hadn't pushed forward, he was standing in the very back, at his ease and rather elegantly dressed, as was his way. His gaze seemed to be directed at the horse's head, and once more it had that profound, quiet, almost fanatical, and yet passionless attentiveness. I had to look at him for some time, and I then sensed—still far from fully conscious of it—something very peculiar. I saw Demian's face, and I saw not merely that he didn't have a boy's face but a man's; more than that, I saw, or I thought I saw or sensed, that it wasn't a man's face, either, but something different still. There seemed to be something of a woman's face in it as well; in short, for a moment that face struck me not as masculine or childlike, not old or young, but somehow millennial, somehow outside of time, bearing the mark of different eons from those we live in. Animals might look like that, or trees, or stars—I didn't know, I didn't precisely feel what I am now, as an adult, saying about it, but I felt something similar. Maybe he was handsome, maybe I liked him, maybe he was repellent to me, too; that couldn't be decided, either. I only saw: he was different from us, he was like an animal, or like a spirit, or like an image; I don't know what he was like, but he was different, inconceivably different from all of us.

More my recollection fails to tell me, and maybe even that much is partly drawn from later impressions.

It was only when I was several years older that I finally came into closer touch with him again. Demian hadn't been confirmed in church with those of his age, as customs might have demanded; and that had immediately given rise to a new set of rumors. Again it was said in school that he was really a Jew—or, no, a heathen—and others were sure that he and his mother had no religion or belonged to some fabulous evil sect. In that connection, I think I also heard the suspicion that he and his mother lived like lovers. Presumably, it was true that until then he had been raised outside of any formal religion, but that this now aroused fears of some difficulties for his future. In any case, his mother decided to let him finally participate in Confirmation, two years later than his age group. That's how it came about that for months he was now my classmate in Confirmation class.

For a while I hung back from him altogether, I didn't want any part of him, he was too enveloped in rumors and mysteries to suit me; but I was especially hindered by the sense of obligation that had stayed with me since the Kromer business. And it was just at that time that my own secrets were all I could handle. For me the Confirmation class coincided with the time of my decisive enlightenment on sexual matters, and despite my good intentions, my interest in pious instruction was severely handicapped by that. The things the clergyman spoke about were located far away from me in a tranquil, holy unreality; they might be very beautiful and valuable, but they were in no way of current interest or stimulating, whereas those other things were just that, and in the highest degree.

The more this situation made me indifferent to my lessons now, the more my interest focused again on Max Demian. Something seemed to tie us together. I must pursue this line of thought with maximum precision. As far as I can recall, it began during one early morning class when lights were still burning in the classroom. The clergyman instructing us had come to the story of Cain and Abel. I was scarcely paying attention, I was sleepy and hardly listening. Then the pastor raised his voice and began to talk forcefully about the mark of Cain. At that moment I sensed a kind of touch or admonition, and, looking up, I saw Demian's face looking back at me from one of the rows of benches closer to the front; the expression in his bright, communicative eyes might just as well have been sarcastic as serious. He looked at me for only a moment, and suddenly I was listening intently to the pastor's words; I heard him talk about Cain and his mark, and deep inside me I felt the knowledge that the way he was teaching this wasn't exactly right, that it could also be taken another way, that it could be critically examined!

At that moment my link to Demian was reinstated. And, strange to say—right after I sensed this kind of solidarity in my soul, I saw it magically transferred to the spatial realm as well. I didn't know if he could arrange it by himself or if it was a pure accident—in those days I still believed firmly in accidental events—a few days later Demian had suddenly changed seats in religion class and was sitting right in front of me (I still recall how gratefully, amid the wretched poorhouse atmosphere of that overcrowded classroom, I inhaled the fresh, sweet smell of soap coming from his neck in the morning!), and a few days after that he had changed again and was now sitting next to me, where he remained seated that entire winter and spring.

The morning classes had been completely transformed. They were no longer soporific and boring. I looked forward to them. Sometimes we both listened to the pastor as attentively as possible; a glance from my neighbor sufficed to indicate a remarkable story or unusual saying to me. And another look from him, a very resolute one, sufficed to put me on my guard, to arouse a spirit of criticism and doubt in me.

But very often we were bad pupils and heard nothing that was being taught. Demian was always polite to his teachers and fellow pupils; I never saw him fool around the way schoolboys do, I never heard him laugh out loud or talk during class; he was never scolded by the teacher. But very quietly, and more with signs and looks than with whispers, he was able to let me have a share in his own preoccupations. Some of these were of an unusual kind.

For instance, he told me which of the pupils interested him, and the way in which he studied them. He knew some of their habits very well. He told me before the lesson: "When I give you a sign with my thumb, So-and-so will look around at us, or scratch the back of his neck," and so forth. Then, during class, when I had almost forgotten all about it, Max suddenly turned his thumb toward me with a conspicuous gesture. I quickly looked at the designated pupil, and each time I saw him, like a marionette on a string, perform the preannounced gesture. I kept Max trying it out on the teacher sometimes, but he always refused. Once, however, when I came to class and told him I hadn't learned my assignment for the day and hoped the pastor wouldn't ask me anything that day, he helped me out. The pastor was looking for a pupil to recite a bit of catechism, and his roving eye lit on my guilty-looking face. He walked over slowly, pointed his finger at me, he already had my name on his lips—when he suddenly became distracted or nervous, tugged at his collar, walked up to Demian, who was staring into his face, and seemed about to ask him something, but surprisingly turned away again, coughed for a while, and then called on another pupil.

I noticed only gradually, while these stunts amused me greatly, that my friend often was playing the same trick on me. On occasion, I suddenly had the feeling on the way to school that Demian was walking a little distance behind me, and when I turned around, he was actually there.

"Can you really make someone else think what you want him to?" I asked him.

He informed me willingly, calmly and objectively, in his grown-up fashion.

"No," he said, "that's impossible. You see, no one has free will, even though the pastor implies that. The other fellow can't think what he wants to, nor can I make him think what I want him to. But it is possible to observe someone carefully, and then you can often say pretty accurately what he's thinking or feeling, and then you can generally foresee what he'll do the next minute. It's quite simple, people just don't know it. Naturally, it takes practice. For example, in the butterfly family, there are certain night moths with a lot fewer females than males. The moths reproduce just as all animals do; the male fertilizes the female, which then lays eggs. Now, when you have a female of this kind of moth—this has often been tested by biologists—the male moths fly to that female at night, and they fly for hours to get there! Just imagine, hours of flying time! Over miles and miles, all these males sense the only female in the vicinity! People try to explain it, but it's hard. It must be some kind of sense of smell or something like that, more or less the way good hunting hounds are able to locate an imperceptible trail and follow it. Understand? There are such things, nature is full of them, and no one can explain them. But now I say: if females occurred as frequently as males among those moths, they wouldn't have that subtle nose! They have it solely because they've trained themselves for it. When an animal or person focuses all his attention and all his willpower on a given objective, he achieves it. That's all there is to it. And it's just the same as what you asked about. Look at a person carefully long enough, and you'll know more about him than he does."

The word "mind-reading" was on the tip of my tongue, and I was about to remind him of the incident with Kromer that had taken place so long before. But this was yet another strange thing in our relationship: never ever did either he or I allude in the slightest way to the fact that once, several years earlier, he had played such a serious part in my life. It was as if there had never been anything between us before, or as if each of us were sure that the other one had forgotten it. Once or twice we even ran across Franz Kromer while walking down the street together, but we didn't exchange a glance or say a word about him.

"But how does that willpower thing work?" I asked. "You say people don't have free will. But then you go on to say that all you need to do is concentrate your willpower on something and you can attain your goal. But that doesn't add up! If I'm not the master of my own will, then I can't focus on any place I choose to."

He tapped me on the shoulder. He always did that when he was pleased with me.

"I'm glad you're asking that!" he said with a smile. "People should always ask questions, they should always entertain doubts. But the matter is very simple. If, for example, a moth of that type wanted to focus its willpower on a star or some such thing, it wouldn't be able to. But it never tries to. It's only out after things that have meaning and value for it, things it needs and absolutely must-have. And then it even accomplishes the unbelievable—it develops a magical sixth sense that no other animal possesses! We human beings have greater latitude, of course, and more interests than an animal does. But we, too, are confined in a relatively small circle and can't go beyond it. I can fantasize about this and that, I can imagine I just must get to the North Pole, or something like that, but I can only accomplish it and will it strongly enough. If the total wish is in my mind, when my being is really completely filled with it. The moment that's the case, the moment you attempt a task that something inside you orders you to do, you'll succeed, you can harness your willpower like a trusty draft horse. For example, if I were now to try and make our pastor leave off wearing glasses, it wouldn't work. That's only a game. But when I decided firmly, back in the fall, to be moved out of my bench in the front of the room, it all went well. Suddenly someone showed up whose name was ahead of mine in the alphabet and who had been ill up to them; and since someone had to yield his seat to him, I was naturally the one who did it, because my will was prepared to seize the opportunity at once."

"Yes," I said, "at the time it struck me as very odd, too. From the moment we got interested in each other, you moved closer and closer to me. But how was it that at first you didn't get to sit right next to me, but started off by sitting on the bench in front of me a few times, right? How was that?"

"It was like this: I wasn't clear about what I wanted, when I felt the urge to move away from my first seat. I only knew I wanted to sit further back. It was my will to come to you, but I had not yet become conscious of it. At the same time your own will pulled along and helped me out. Only when I was sitting in front of you did it occur to me that my wish was only half-fulfilled—I noticed that my desire had really only been to sit next to you."

"But at that time no new boy entered the class."

"No, but that time I simply did what I wanted, and just sat down next to you. The boy with whom I changed places was merely surprised and let me have my way. And the pastor did notice once that a change had taken place—in general, whenever he has dealings with me, something nags at him secretly, because he knows my name is Demian and it isn't right for me, with my name beginning with D, to be sitting all the way in the back among the S's! But that doesn't reach his consciousness because my will is set against it and I prevent him time and again from becoming aware of it. Each time he notices that something is wrong, he looks at me and starts to ponder, the dear man. But I have a simple remedy. Each time, I stare really hard into his eyes. Almost no one can abide by that. Everyone gets nervous. If you want to get something out of anybody, and he doesn't get nervous when you unexpectedly stare hard into his eyes, give up. You won't get anything out of him, never! But that's very rare. Actually I know only one person that doesn't work for me."

"Who is that?" I asked quickly.

He looked at me with those partially narrowed eyes that were a sign he was reflecting on something. Then he looked away and made no reply, and despite my overpowering curiosity, I couldn't repeat the question.

But I think he meant his mother when he said that. He seemed to have a very warm relationship with her, but he never spoke to me about her and never brought me home with him. I scarcely knew what his mother looked like.

Sometimes in those days, I made attempts to imitate him and to concentrate my willpower on some goal so hard that I had to achieve it. I had wishes that seemed urgent enough to me. But nothing came of it; it didn't work. I couldn't bring myself to discuss it with Demian. I couldn't have confessed to him what sort of things I was wishing for. Nor did he ask.

My belief when it came to religion had frittered away in the meantime. But in my way of thinking, which was totally influenced by Demian, I differed greatly from those among my fellow pupils who displayed total disbelief. There were some such, and occasionally they made remarks to the effect that it was ridiculous and beneath human I dignity to believe in a God; that stories like those of the Trinity and Jesus's immaculate birth were simply laughable; and that it was a shame to peddle such junk in this day and age. That's not at all what I thought. Even when I had doubts, I still knew enough from the whole experience of my childhood about the reality of a pious life such as my parents led, for instance; I knew it was neither unworthy nor hypocritical. Instead, I constantly retained the most profound respect for religiosity. Only, Demian had accustomed me to look on, and to interpret, the stories and the articles of faith in a freer, more personal, less rigid, more imaginative way; at least I always followed the interpretations he suggested to me gladly and with enjoyment. To be sure, many things were too brutal for me, including that business with Cain. And once during our Confirmation lessons he frightened me with a conception that was possibly even more daring. The teacher had spoken about Golgotha. Since my earliest days the Bible story of the Passion and death of the Savior had made a strong impression on me; sometimes when I was small, say on Good Friday, after my father had read aloud the story of the Passion, I had lived, warmly and with sincere sympathy, in that sorrowfully beautiful, pale, ghostly, and yet tremendously alive world, in Gethsemane and on Golgotha; and when I heard Bach's St Matthew Passion, the soberly powerful glow of sorrow from that mysterious world had washed over me with all its mystical thrills. Even today I find in that composition, and in the Actus Tragicus,[4] the embodiment of all poetry and all artistic expression.

Now, at the close of that lesson, Demian said to me reflectively: "Sinclair, there's something in this I don't like. Just read the story over again and test it out on your tongue; it's got something that tastes insipid, namely that business with the two thieves. It's splendid the way the three crosses stand side by side on the hill! But then comes that sentimental story with the upright thief, right out of some cheap religious pamphlet! First, he was a criminal and committed shameful deeds, God knows what all,

4. One commentator states that Actus Tragicus is merely another term for Christ's Passion, but in the context it must refer to Bach's Cantata 106, which is known by that name as well as by its opening words, "Gottes Zeit ist die allerbeste Zeit."

and now he melts away and performs lachrymose rites about mending his ways and repenting! What's the sense of that kind of repentance two steps away from the grave, I ask you? It's just another story right out of a sermon, saccharine and dishonest, tugging sentimentally at your heartstrings, with a highly edifying background. If today you had to choose one of the two thieves as a friend or think about which of the two you could sooner put your trust in, it's certainly not that whimpering convert. No, it's the other one; he's a real man with character. He doesn't give a hoot about converting, which in his situation can only be pretty speechifying; he travels his path to the end, and doesn't act like a coward at the last minute, renouncing the Devil, who must have helped him up till then. He's a man of character, and people of character generally get short shrift in Bible stories. Maybe he's a descendant of Cain. Don't you think so?"

I was quite dismayed. I had thought I was right at home here in the story of the Crucifixion, and only now did I see with what little personal involvement, with what little power of imagination and vision I had listened to it and read it. And yet Demian's new idea sounded awful to me; it threatened to overthrow concepts in my mind that I thought I had to retain. No, it was wrong to treat everything so casually, even the most sacred things.

He noticed my resistance immediately, as always, even before I said anything.

"I know, I know," he said with an air of resignation, "it's the old story. Anything but be serious! But I want to tell you something: Here is one of the places where the shortcomings in this religion can be seen very clearly. The fact is that this whole God, both in the Old and the New Testament, may be an outstanding figure, but He's not what He should really represent. He is goodness, nobility, the Father, beauty and also loftiness, sentimentality—all fine!

But the world is made up of other things, too. And all that is simply ascribed to the Devil, and this whole part of the world, an entire half, is swept under the table and buried in silence. In the same way, they praise God as the Father of all life, but when it comes to sex life, on which life after all depends, they simply bury it in silence and as much as possible declare it to be sinful, the work of the Devil! I have nothing against honoring this God Jehovah, not in the least. But my opinion is that we should honor everything and hold it sacred, the whole world, not just this artificially detached, official half! And so, alongside the divine service for God, we must also have a service for the Devil. I think that would be proper. Or else, people would have to create some new God, who would also include the Devil within Himself, one in whose presence we wouldn't have to shut our eyes when the most natural things in the world take place."

Contrary to his nature, he had grown nearly stormy, but immediately afterward he smiled again and didn't pursue the matter further with me.

But in my mind those words struck home to the riddle of my entire childhood, the riddle I carried inside me hourly and I had never told anyone about. What Demian had then said about God and the Devil, about the divinely official world and the devilish world buried in silence, was precisely my own idea, my own myth, the idea of the two worlds or the two halves of the world, the bright and the dark. The insight that my problem was a problem of all mankind, a problem of all life and thought, suddenly passed over me like a sacred shadow; and fear and reverence overpowered me when I saw and suddenly felt how profoundly my very own personal life and opinions shared in the eternal stream of great ideas. This insight was not joyous, even though it somehow made me happy by confirming my opinions. It was tough and tasted raw, because it contained a note of responsibility, of the necessity to cease being a child and to stand on my own feet.

Revealing such a deep secret for the first time in my life, I told my comrade about that conception of the "two worlds" that had been with me since earliest childhood; and he saw at once that my deepest emotions were thereby in harmony and agreement with his. But it wasn't his way to exploit such a revelation. He listened with greater attentiveness than he had ever before given me, and looked into my eyes until I had to avert them. Because I once again saw in his gaze that strange, animal—like timelessness, that inconceivable antiquity.

"We'll talk more about it another time," he said considerately. "I see that you think more than you can express. But, if that's the case, you must also know that you have never fully lived out your thoughts, and that isn't good. Only the thoughts that we live out have any value. You knew that your 'permissible world' was only half the world, and you tried to hide away the second half from yourself, the way clergymen and teachers do. You won't succeed! No one can do that when he has once begun to think."

That made a strong impression on me.

I nearly yelled: "But there really and truly are forbidden, ugly things, you can't deny it! And they're definitely forbidden, and we have to renounce them. I know that murder and all possible vices exist, but shall I, merely because they exist, go out and become a criminal?"

"We won't get to the bottom of it today," Max said, pacifying me. "Certainly you mustn't commit murder or kill girls after raping them, no. But you haven't yet reached the stage where people can tell what 'permitted' and 'forbidden' really mean. So far you've only sensed a part of the truth. The rest will follow, rely on it! Now, for example, since about a year ago, you have a drive within you that's stronger than all others, and it's supposed to be 'forbidden.' On the other hand, the Greeks and many other nations made a deity of that drive and honored it with great festivals. And so 'forbidden' isn't something eternal, it can change. Today, too, any man can sleep with a woman as soon as he's taken her to the person and married her. It's different among other people, even to this day. Therefore each of us must discover for himself what is permitted and what is forbidden—forbidden to him. It's possible for someone never to do any forbidden thing, and yet be a thorough scoundrel. And vice versa. Actually, it's merely a question of convenience! Whoever is too comfortable-loving to do his own thinking and be his own judge simply adapts to the pre-existing negative commandments. It's easy for him. Others feel commandments of their own within themselves; for them things are forbidden which every respectable man does daily, and other things are permissible for them which are normally tabooed. Everyone must stand on his own feet."

Suddenly he seemed to regret having said that much, and he broke off. Even then I could already grasp with my emotions to some extent what he was feeling at the time. You see, no matter how pleasantly and apparently offhandedly he was accustomed to expressing his ideas, nevertheless, he hated to converse "just for the sake of talking," as he once put it. But he sensed that, alongside my genuine interest, I was too playful, taking too much pleasure in clever babbling or the like; in short, that I lacked total seriousness.

On rereading the last words I wrote, "total seriousness," I suddenly recall another scene, the most memorable one I experienced with Max in those days when I was still half a child.

Our Confirmation was approaching, and the final lessons of our religious instruction dealt with Communion. The person took the subject seriously and took pains with it; an element of consecration and uplifting atmosphere could easily be discerned in those lessons. But precisely during those last few lessons, my thoughts were occupied elsewhere, namely with my friend's personality. While I approached Confirmation, which was explained to us as our solemn reception into the community of the Church, the idea rose up irrepressibly in my mind that for me the value of that religious instruction, which had lasted about half a year, lay not in what we had learned there, but in Demian's nearness and influence. It was not into the Church that I was now ready to receive, but into something quite different, into a select society of thought and personality which had to exist somewhere on earth, an order whose representative or envoy I took my friend to be.

I tried to repress those thoughts; I was serious about experiencing the celebration of Confirmation with a certain dignity, despite everything, and this dignity seemed to harmonize badly with my new thoughts. But, do what. I might, the thought was there, and it gradually became connected in my mind with the thought of the forthcoming church ritual; I was prepared to celebrate it differently from the rest; for me it was to signify the reception into a world of thought such as I had become acquainted within the person of Demian.

It was in those days that I once again had a lively argument with him; it was precisely before one of those lessons. My friend was reserved and took no pleasure in what I said, which was probably rather precocious and self-important.

"We're talking too much," he said with unaccustomed gravity. "Smart talk has no value, none at all. It just leads you away from yourself. To depart from yourself is a sin. A person must be able to crawl away into himself completely, like a turtle."

Right after that we entered the classroom. The lesson began, I tried hard to pay attention, and Demian didn't hinder me. After a while I began to get a strange feeling on the side where he was sitting next to me; it was a void or a chill or something of the sort, as if the seat had become empty unexpectedly. When the feeling began to become oppressive, I turned around.

There I saw my friend sitting, erect and with good posture as always. But all the same, he looked altogether different than usual, and something emanated from him, something enveloped him, that I was unfamiliar with. I thought he had shut his eyes, but I saw they were open. But they weren't looking at anything, they were sightless, they were rigid, directed inwardly or into a great distance. He sat there totally motionless; he didn't seem to be breathing, either; his mouth looked as if it were carved out of wood or stone. His face was pale, uniformly pallid, like stone, and his brown hair was the most living thing about him. His hands lay in front of him on the bench, as lifeless and still as objects, as stones or fruits, pallid and motionless, but not limp; rather, like good, firm husks protecting a strong hidden life.

The sight made me tremble. "He's dead!" I thought; I almost said it out loud. But I knew he wasn't dead. With spellbound eyes, I stared at his face, at that pale stone mask, and I felt: that was Demian! His usual manner, when he walked and talked with me, was only half of Demian, one playing a temporary role, adapting himself, obligingly sharing my existence. But the real Demian looked like that, like this person, just as stony, age-old, animal-like, stonelike, beautiful and cold, dead and secretly filled with unimaginable life. And around him this silent void, this ether and celestial space, this solitary death!

Now he has withdrawn completely into himself, I felt as if I trembled. I had never been so all alone. I had no part in him, he was inaccessible to me, he was farther away from me than if he had been on the remotest island in the world. '

I scarcely comprehended that no one saw it except me! Everyone should be looking this way, everyone should be trembling at the sight! But no one gave him any heed. He sat there stiff as a statue and, as I was forced to think, stiff as an idol; a fly settled on his forehead and walked slowly over his nose and lips—not one crease of his skin twitched.

Where, where was he now? What was he thinking, what was he feeling? Was he in some heaven, some hell?

It wasn't possible for me to ask him about it. At the end of the lesson, when I saw him living and breathing again, when his eyes met mine, he was as before. From where was he returning? Where had he been? He seemed tired. His face had color again, his hands were moving again, but his brown hair had now lost its sheen and seemed weary.

In the days that followed I devoted myself several times to a new exercise in my bedroom: I sat down stiffly on a chair, made my eyes rigid, kept completely motionless, and waited to see how long I could keep it up and how it would affect me. But I only got tired, and my eyelids started to itch violently.

Shortly thereafter I was confirmed; I'm left with no significant memories of that occasion.

Now everything has become different. Childhood fell away from me in ruins. My parents beheld me with a certain embarrassment. My sisters had become total strangers to me. A sense of sobriety falsified my customary emotions and pleasures, draining them of substance; the garden had no fragrance, the forest didn't attract me, the world around me was like a clearance sale of shopworn merchandise, insipid and unappealing, books were just paper, music just a noise. In just such a way the leaves fall around a tree in autumn; the tree doesn't feel it, the rain trickles down it, or sunshine, or frost, and within its life slowly retreats into its narrowest, inmost recesses. It doesn't die. It waits.

It had been decided that after summer vacation I would attend another school and leave home for the first time. At times my mother approached me with particular tenderness, taking leave of me in advance, striving to conjure love, homesickness, and a lack of forgetfulness into my heart. Demian had gone out of town. I was alone.

CHAPTER 4

BEATRICE

Without having seen my friend again, at the end of the vacation I traveled to St—. Both my parents came along and with all possible care entrusted me to the protection of a boys' boarding house run by a teacher at the secondary school. They would have frozen with horror, had they known what kind of life they were now letting me drift into.

The question was still whether with time I could become a good son and useful citizen, or whether my nature urged me onto other paths. My latest attempt at happiness within the shadow of my father's house and spirit had lasted a long time, had occasionally been almost successful, and yet had completely failed at the end.

The strange emptiness and solitude I had first come to feel during the vacation after my Confirmation (how familiar I was to become with it later on, that emptiness, that rarefied atmosphere!) didn't pass away so quickly. Saying goodbye to my home came oddly easily to me, I was actually ashamed at not being gloomier; my sisters cried for no particular reason, but I couldn't. I was surprised at myself. I had always been an affectionate child, and basically a rather good child. Now I was completely transformed.

I acted totally indifferent to the world outside and for days on end was only concerned with listening to myself, with hearing the streams, the forbidden, dark streams that resounded within me beneath the surface. I had grown taller very quickly, all within the last half-year, and it was a gangly, skinny, half-baked youth who looked out onto the world. Boyish charm had vanished from me altogether, I felt that no one could love me as I was, and I didn't like myself one bit. I often missed Max Demian badly; but not infrequently I hated him, too, and blamed him for the impoverishment of my life, which I took upon myself like a loathsome disease.

In our schoolboys' boardinghouse, I was at first neither liked nor respected; first I was teased, then they left me alone and considered me to be a hypocrite and an unpleasant outsider. I enjoyed the role, and even exaggerated it, becoming a loner out of resentment; on the outside my solitude constantly resembled the manliest contempt for the world, whereas in secret I was often subject to debilitating attacks of melancholy and despair. At school I was able to draw upon the knowledge I had accumulated back home; my class was behindhand compared to my old one, and I got used to regarding the boys of my age somewhat contemptuously as children.

Things continued that way for a year and more; even my first trips home during holidays added no new note; I was glad to leave again.

It was at the beginning of November. I had grown accustomed to taking short walks to think things over, no matter what the weather was; on these walks, I often enjoyed a sort of rapture, a rapture filled with melancholy and with contempt for the world and myself. And so I was sauntering one evening in the damp, misty twilight through the outskirts of town; the broad, tree-lined avenue of a public park was completely deserted and invited me to walk there; the path was heaped high with fallen leaves into which I borrowed my toes with an obscure desire; there was a damp, bitter smell; the trees in the distance emerged from the mist as tall and shadowy as ghosts.

At the end of the avenue, I halted undecidedly, stared at the black foliage, and lustily inhaled the damp aroma of decay and death, which something in me responded to and welcomed. Dh, how insipid life tasted!

From a side path, a person in a fluttering collared coat approached; I was about to walk away when he called me.

"Hello, Sinclair!"

He came up to me; it was Alfons Beck, the oldest boy in our boarding house. I was always glad to see him and had nothing against him, except that he was always sarcastic and patronizing to me, as he was to all boys younger than himself. He was said to be strong as a bear and to have the master of our boarding house under his thumb, and he was the hero of many tales in our secondary-school gossip.

"What are you doing here?" he called sociably in the tone the older boys were affected when they occasionally condescended to address one of us. "Yes, I bet you're writing poetry!"

"Never entered my mind," I contradicted him gruffly.

He laughed, walked alongside me, and chatted in a way I was no longer used to.

"You don't have to be afraid that I might not understand you, Sinclair. I know a person is affected when he walks around in the mist like this in the evening, with thoughts of autumn; then he's inclined to write poetry, I know. About dying nature, naturally, and about lost youth, which resembles it. Take Henrich Heine."

"I'm not that sentimental," I said in my defense.

"Well, let that go! But I think that in this weather it's a good idea to seek out a quiet place where you can get a glass of wine or something. Do you want to join me? I happen to be all alone. Or would you rather not? I don't want to be your tempter, my friend, in case you want to be a model boy."

Soon afterward we were sitting in a little suburban tavern, drinking wine of dubious quality and clinking our thick glasses together. At first, I didn't like it much, but at any rate, it was something new. But soon, being unused to wine, I became very talkative. It was as if a window had opened inside me, letting the world shine in—how long, how terribly long it had been since I had gotten anything off my chest! Eventually, I began rambling on, and in the thick of it I trotted out the story of Cain and Abel!

Beck listened to me with pleasure—at last someone, I could give something to! He tapped me on the shoulder, he called me a hell of a guy, and my heart was swelling with bliss at being able to pour out lavishly words and communications which I had needed to speak but which had been dammed up; bliss at being accepted as a companion and holding my own to some extent with older youth. When he called me a clever dog, the phrase coursed through me like sweet, strong wine. The world was glowing in new colors, ideas flowed into my mind from a hundred bubbling springs, the flame of intellect blazed up in me. We talked about our teachers and schoolmates, and I thought we were getting on splendidly. We talked about the Greeks and pagan culture, and Beck tried hard to make me own up to erotic adventures. There I was unable to participate. I had had no experiences, nothing that could be told. What I had felt, devised, or imagined in my mind was burning inside me, to be sure, but even the wine hadn't set it free to be discussed. Beck knew much more about girls, and I listened to those tales passionately. I learned incredible things on that occasion; things I never thought possibly entered my dull existence and seemed self-evident. Alfons Beck, who was perhaps eighteen, had already gathered knowledge. Among other things, he had learned that the trouble with girls was that they wanted nothing but flattery and attention, which was perfectly fine, but not the essential thing. Greater success could be expected with grown women. Women were much cleverer. For example, Mrs. Jaggelt, who owned the store with notebooks and pencils, was a woman you could talk to, and the things that had taken place behind her counter couldn't be printed.

I sat there under a deep spell, stupefied. To be sure, I wouldn't exactly have been able to love Mrs. Jaggelt—but anyway, it was amazing. Opportunities seemed to be available, at least for the older boys, that I had never dreamed of. Yes, there was a false note in this, and it all tasted cheaper and more common than love ought to taste in my opinion—but anyway, it was reality, it was life and adventure; someone was sitting next to me who had experienced it, to whom it seemed self-evident.

Our conversation had lowered its tone somewhat, it had lost some quality. And I was no longer the clever little guy; now I was still just a boy listening to a man. But even so-compared with what my life had been for months and months, this was priceless, this was heavenly. Besides, as I only now gradually began to feel, it was forbidden, strictly forbidden, from sitting in a tavern to our current topic of conversation. At any rate, I found in it a taste of intellect, a taste of revolution.

I remember that night extremely distinctly. When the two of us started walking home in the chilly, damp late night, passing the dimly burning gas street lamps, I was drunk for the first time. It wasn't pleasant, it was extremely distressing, and yet even that had something to it, an attraction, a sweetness; it was rebellion and orgy, it was life and intellect. Beck took charge of me valiantly, though he cursed me bitterly as a raw novice, and, half-carrying me, he brought me home, where he managed to sneak me and himself through an open vestibule window.

But when I was sober, waking up after a very brief dead sleep, an unreasoning sorrow overcame me. I sat up in bed, still wearing my daytime shirt; my clothes and shoes were scattered on the floor and smelled of tobacco and vomit; and between the headache, nausea, and a wild thirst an image arose in my mind that I hadn't faced up to for a long time. I saw my hometown and my parents' house, my father and mother, sisters and garden; I saw my quiet, homey bedroom, I saw my school and Market Square, I saw Demian and our Confirmation lessons—and all of that was bright, it was all surrounded by radiance, it was all wonderful, divine, and pure; and all, all of that—I knew it now—had belonged to me and had been waiting for me only yesterday, only hours ago; and now, just now at that moment, it had sunk out of sight and was accursed; it no longer belonged to me, it cast me out, it looked on me with disgust! All the love and warmth my parents had shown me since the remotest, most golden gardens of my childhood, every kiss from my mother, every Christmas, every pious, bright Sunday morning at home, every flower in the garden—it was all ravaged, I had trampled on it all! If bailiffs had come at that moment, tied my hands, and led me to the gallows as an outcast and a defiler of the Temple, I would have agreed to it, I would have gone gladly, I would have considered it proper and right.

That, then, was how I looked on the inside! I, who went around despising the world! I, who was proud in mind and shared some ideas with Demian! That's how I looked, an outcast, a dirty pig, drunk and filthy, disgusting and common, a dissolute beast, caught unawares by my horrible impulses! That's how I looked. I came from those gardens where everything was purity, radiance, and loving tenderness. I loved music by Bach and beautiful poems! It was with disgust and rage that I still heard my own laughter, a burst of drunken, uncontrolled laughter that broke out in fits and sounded stupid. That's who I was!

But, despite everything, it was almost a pleasure to suffer those torments. I had crawled through life blindly and dully for so long, my heart had kept silent and had sat, impoverished, in a corner for so long, that even these self-accusations, this horror, this whole ghastly emotion in my soul was welcome. After all, it was an emotion, flames were still rising, it showed that my heart was still alive! In a confused way, in the midst of my misery, I felt something like liberation and springtime.

Meanwhile, viewed from the outside, things were going decidedly downhill with me. My first binge was soon no longer the only one. At our school there was a lot of tavern going and tomfoolery; I was one of the very youngest among those who joined in, and soon I was no longer a youngster who was merely tolerated, but a leader and chief, a notorious, reckless tavern goer. Once again I belonged wholly to the dark world, to the Devil, and in that world, I counted as a great guy.

But as I did so, I felt terrible. My life drifted by a self-destructive orgy, and while I was looked on by my schoolmates as a leader and a hell of a guy, a damned plucky and witty fellow, deep inside me my anxiety-ridden soul was shaking with alarm. I still recall that tears once came to my eyes when I stepped out of a tavern one Sunday morning and saw children playing in the street, bright and happy, with hair just combed and in their Sunday best. And while I was sitting among pools of beer at dirty tables in cheap taverns, entertaining and often frightening my friends with unusually cynical remarks, deep in my heart I revered everything I was mocking, and in my mind, I was weeping on my knees before my soul, my past, my mother, and God.

If I never was at one with my companions, if I remained solitary in their company and was thus able to suffer this way, there was a good reason for it. I was a saloon goer and cynic to suit the most vulgar people, I displayed wit and courage in what I thought and said about our teachers, school, parents, church—I even tolerated dirty jokes and occasionally dared to tell some of my own—but I was never alone when my buddies visited girls; I was alone and filled with ardent longing for love, hopeless longing, while to judge by what I said, I'd have to have been a veteran playboy. No one was more vulnerable or shy than I was. And when I occasionally saw young middle-class girls walking by me, pretty and clean, bright and graceful, they were wonderful, pure; 'I dream in my eyes, thousand times too good and pure for me. For a time I couldn't even go back to Mrs. Jagger's stationery store, because I blushed whenever I saw her and thought about what Alfons Beck had told me about her.

The more I felt constantly alone and different, even in my new circle of friends, the more unable I was to break away. I no longer recall whether drinking and boasting ever actually gave me pleasure; besides, I never got so used to alcohol that I didn't suffer painful consequences every time I drank. It was all like a compulsion. I did what I had to, because otherwise I simply had no idea what to do with myself. I was afraid of being alone for long periods; I stood in fear of the numerous tender, shy, warm impulses toward which I constantly felt responsive; I stood in fear of the tender thoughts of love that came to me so frequently.

One thing I missed above all—a friend. There were two or three fellow students whose company I enjoyed a lot. But they were among the well-behaved, and for some time my vices had been no secret to anyone. They avoided me. They all regarded me as a desperate gambler who was losing his footing. The teachers knew a lot about me, I had been severely punished several times, my definitive expulsion was expected. I knew it; besides, by that time I had long ceased to be a good student, but painfully squeezed and cheated my way through, with the feeling that things couldn't go on that way very long.

There are many ways in which God can make us lonely and lead us to ourselves. He took that path with me in those days. It was like a bad dream. I see myself, spellbound in a dream, restless and in torment, crawling along with past slimy filth, broken beer glasses, and nights of cynical conversation, an ugly, unclean path. There are dreams in which you are on the way to meet a princess but get bogged down in puddles of excrement, in back alleys reeking with garbage. That's how it was with me. It was my lot, in this indelicate way, to grow lonely, and to erect between me and my childhood a locked door to Eden with mercilessly flaming guardians. It was a beginning, an awakening of homesickness for myself.

I still got frightened and felt twinges when my father, alarmed by letters from the teacher who ran my boardinghouse, first appeared in S— unexpectedly walked up to me. When, toward the end of that winter, he came a second time, I was already hardened and indifferent; I let him scold me, let him plead with me, let him remind me of my mother. Finally, he got very worked up and said that, if I didn't change my ways, he would let me be kicked out of school in disgrace and would put me in a reform school. Well, let him! When he departed that time, I felt sorry for him, but he hadn't accomplished a thing, he hadn't been able to reach me anymore, and for a while, I felt that it served him right.

I didn't care what would become of me. In my peculiar and unlovely way, I was at war with the world when I sat in taverns and bragged; it was my form of protest. By doing so I was ruining myself, and at times my prospects were more or less as follows: if the world couldn't use people like me, if it had no better place or higher goals for them, then people like me just went to rack and ruin. Let the world suffer the consequences.

Christmas vacation that year was almost unenjoyable. My mother got scared when she saw me again. I had grown even taller, and my thin face looked gray and ravaged, with limp features and red-rimmed eyes. The first hint of a moustache, and the eyeglasses I had recently started to wear, made me even more unfamiliar to her. My sisters hung back and giggled. Everything was unpleasant. Unpleasant and bitter the conversation with my father in his study, unpleasant greeting from the handful of relatives, unpleasant, above all, Christmas Eve. All my life that had been the great day in our house, the evening of festivity and love, of gratitude, of renewing the bond between my parents and myself. This time everything was merely oppressive and embarrassing. As usual, my father read aloud from the Gospel the passage about the shepherds in the fields "watching their flocks by night"; as usual my sisters stood radiantly in front of their table of presents, but my father's voice sounded unhappy, and his face looked old and gaunt, and my mother was sad, and to me, everything was equally painful and unwanted, gifts and good wishes, Gospel and lighted tree. The gingerbread smelt sweet and gave off dense clouds of sweeter memories. The Christmas tree was aromatic and told of things that no longer existed. I longed for the end of the evening and the vacation.

Things continued that way all winter. Only shortly before, I had received a drastic warning from the council of teachers and had been threatened with expulsion. It wouldn't last much longer. Well, what did I care about?

I had a special grudge against Max Demian. I hadn't seen him again in all that time. At the beginning of my school days in St— I had written to him twice, but never got an answer; for that reason I hadn't visited him during my vacation, either.

In the same park where I had run across Alfons Beck in the fall, it happened at the beginning of spring, just when the hawthorn hedges were beginning to get green, that a girl caught my attention. I had gone out for a walk alone, filled with repellent thoughts and worries, because my health worse gotten bad and, in addition, I was constantly in financial difficulties; I owed sums to schoolmates, I had to invent the urgent need to purchase supplies in order to get more money from home, and I had allowed bills for cigars and such to pile up in several stores. Not that these worries went very deep—whenever, in the near future, my stay here came to an end and I either drowned myself or was sent to reform school, these few trifles would hardly matter. But, all the same, I lived in a constant view of such unpleasantness and I suffered from it.

On that spring day in the park, I met a young lady who attracted me very much. She was tall and slender, elegantly dressed, and had an intelligent, boyish face. I liked her at once, she was of the type that I loved, and she began to occupy my daydreams. She was probably scarcely older than I was, but much more mature, elegant and with clear contours, already almost a total lady, but with a hint of high spirits and boyishness in her face that I especially liked.

I had never succeeded in approaching a girl I felt attracted to, and I didn't succeed in her case, either. But the impression she made was stronger than on any prior occasion, and the influence this infatuation had on my life was powerful.

Suddenly I once more had an image before me, a lofty, revered image—and, oh! there was no need, no urge within me as strong and vehement as my wish to respect and venerate something! I gave her the name Beatrice, because, without having read Dante, I knew about her from an English painting,[5] a reproduction of which I had kept. It was an English Pre-Raphaelite figure of a girl, slender, with very long limbs and a long, narrow face and spiritual hands and features. My beautiful young girl didn't resemble her exactly, though she, too, displayed that slenderness and boyishness of forms that I loved, and something of that spirituality and soulfulness in the face.

I never said a single word to Beatrice. And yet she exerted the strongest influence on me in those days. She held up her image before me, she opened a shrine for me, she made me a worshipper in a temple. From one day to the next, I began to stay away from taverns going and roaming the streets at night in a gang. I was able to be alone again, I once more enjoyed reading and taking walks.

This sudden conversion made me the butt of plenty of jokes. But now I had something to love and adore, I once again had an idea; life was once again filled with presentations and a mysterious, variegated twilight glow. And that made me insensitive to scorn. Once more I felt at home with myself, although only as a slave and servant of a venerated image.

I can't think back to that time without some tender emotion. I was trying again with the most ardent efforts to construct a "bright world" for myself from the ruins of a period in my life

5. Beata Beatrix, by Dante Gabriel Rossetti, 1863.

that had collapsed; again I was living altogether in the one and only desire to cast away what was dark and evil in me, and to dwell entirely in the light, kneeling before gods. Anyway, this present "bright world" was to some extent my own creation; it no longer meant taking refuge and crawling back to my mother and a sheltered life devoid of responsibility, but a new service that I had invented and demanded, with responsibility and self-discipline. My sexuality, from which I suffered and was always trying to escape, was now to be transfigured into spirit and worship in this sacred fire. There must no longer be any darkness, any ugliness, any nights spent in moaning, any palpitations of the heart when looking at dirty pictures, any listening at forbidden doors, any lust. In place of all that, I set up my altar, with the picture of Beatrice, and as I consecrate myself to her, I consecrate myself to spirit and the gods. The portion of my life that I snatched away from the forces of darkness, I sacrificed to the forces of light. My goal was not pleasure, but purity; not happiness, but beauty and intellectuality.

This cult of Beatrice altered my life entirely. Only yesterday a precocious cynic, I was now a Temple servant whose goal was to become a saint. I not only cast off the evil ways I had become accustomed to, I tried to change everything; I tried to bring purity, nobility, and dignity into everything, keeping this in mind in the way I ate, drank, spoke, and dressed. I started off the day with cold ablutions, which at first I had to force myself strenuously to perform. My behavior was serious and dignified, I bore myself erect and walked at a slower and more dignified pace. It may have seemed funny to onlookers—in my mind, it was sheer divine service.

Of all the new practices in which I sought expression for my new frame of mind, one became important to me. I began to paint. It started with my finding that the English picture of Beatrice I owned didn't sufficiently resemble that girl I used to see. I wanted to try and paint her for myself. With a brand-new joy and hope I assembled in my room—I had recently moved into a room of my own—fine paper, paints, and brushes, and I prepared a palette, glass, porcelain dishes, and pencils. The fine tempera colors in little tubes that I had bought delighted me. Among them was a fiery chrome green that I still seem to see as it first gleamed in the little white dish.

I began cautiously. To paint a face was hard; I wanted to attempt something else first. I painted ornaments, flowers, and little imaginary landscapes, a tree by a chapel, a Roman bridge with cypresses. At times I became completely absorbed in that playful activity; I was as happy as a child with a box of paints. But finally, I began to paint Beatrice.

Some sheets were total failures and were thrown out. The harder I tried to picture to myself the face of the girl whom I met on the street from time to time, the less success I had. Finally, I gave up and simply started painting a face, following my imagination and the leads spontaneously furnished by my first strokes, by the paint and the brush. It was a dream face that resulted, and I was not unsatisfied with it. But I continued the experiment at once, and each new sheet spoke a little more distinctly, coming closer to the type, although not at all to the reality.

I grew more and more accustomed to drawing lines and filling in surfaces with a dreamy brush; these lines and surfaces had no model but were produced by playful groping, from my unconscious mind. Finally, one day, almost unconsciously I completed a face that spoke to me more urgently than the earlier ones had. It wasn't the face of that girl; for some time that hadn't been my intention. It was something different, something unreal, but no less valuable. It looked more like a young man's face than a girl's; the hair wasn't light blonde like my pretty girl's, but brown with a reddish tinge; the chin was strong and firm, but the mouth like a red flower; the whole thing was a little stiff and masklike, but impressive and full of a secret life.

When I sat down in front of the finished picture, it made a strange impression on me. It seemed to me like a sort of divine image or sacred mask, half-male, half-female, ageless, equally strong-willed and dreamy, rigid yet secretly alive. That face had something to say to me, it belonged to me, it made demands on me. And it resembled somebody, I didn't know whom.

For some time after that, the portrait accompanied all my thoughts and shared my life. I kept it hidden in a drawer; I didn't want anyone to lay hands on it and use it to mock me. But as soon as I was alone in my little room, I pulled out the picture and it kept me company. In the evening I would pin it to the wallpaper over my bed, facing me, I'd look at it till I fell asleep, and it was the first thing I saw in the morning.

In that same period, I started to have lots of dreams again, just as I had always had in my childhood. It seemed as if I hadn't dreamt for years. Now the dreams returned, an entirely new set of images; very often the portrait I had painted showed up in them, living and speaking, friendly or hostile to me, sometimes twisted into a grimace and sometimes infinitely beautiful, harmonious, and noble.

And one morning, as I awoke from such dreams, I suddenly recognized it. It looked at me as a face so enormously well-known, it seemed to be calling my name. It seemed to know me as a mother does, it seemed as if it had been interested in my doings for all eternity, My heart pounding, I stared at the sheet, at the thick brown hair, the half-feminine mouth, the strong forehead that was peculiarly bright (it had dried that way on its own), and I felt recognition, rediscovery, knowledge growing nearer and nearer in me.

I jumped out of bed, stood in front of the face, and looked at it from as close as possible, right into the wide-open, greenish, fixed eyes, of which the right was somewhat higher than the left and all at once that right eye twitched, a light and subtle twitch, but a distinct one, and as it twitched I recognized the picture...

Why had it taken me so long to discover it? It was Demian's face.

Later I often compared the picture with Demian's actual features, as I found them in my memory. They weren't the same, but similar. Yet it was Demian.

On one evening in early summer, the sun was sending oblique red rays through my window, which faced west. Twilight gathered in the room. Then I hit on the notion of pinning the portrait of Beatrice, or Demian, to the cross formed by the window frame, and to look at it as the evening sun shone through it. The face was blurry, without contours, but the red-rimmed eyes, the brightness on the forehead, and the violently red mouth glowed strongly and wildly from the surface. I sat facing it for some time, even after it had grown dark. And gradually I got the feeling that it wasn't Beatrice or Demian, but—myself. The picture didn't resemble me—nor was it meant to, I thought—but it depicted that which constituted my life, it was my inner self, my fate, or my daemon. That's how my friend would look if I ever found one again. That's how my beloved would look if I ever won her. That's how my life and death would be, this was the sound and rhythm of my fate.

In those weeks I had begun reading a book that made a stronger impression on me than anything I had yet read. Even later on,

I seldom had such an experience with books, except perhaps with Nietzsche. It was a volume of Novalis, with letters and aphorisms, many of which I didn't understand, though they all had a marvelous, spellbinding attraction for me. Now one of the sayings occurred to me. I wrote it in ink under the portrait: "A man's fate and his character are two names for the same concept." Now I have understood it.

I still often ran across the girl I called Beatrice. I no longer felt any agitation when I did, but always a gentle harmony of minds, an emotional presentiment: you are linked to me, but not yourself, only your picture; you are a portion of my fate.

My longing for Max Demian grew strong again. I knew nothing of his doings, and hadn't for years. Only once I had met him during vacation. I now see that I have omitted this brief meeting in these memoirs, and I see that I did so out of shame and vanity. I must make up for it and relate to it now.

Well, then, once during vacation, wearing the blasé and constantly somewhat world—weary expression I affected during my drinking days, I was sauntering through my hometown, swinging my walking stick and looking at the same old, unchanged, despised faces of the "Philistine" burghers, when I ran across my former friend. As soon as I saw him, I cringed. And, quick as a flash, I was forced to recall Franz Kromer. If only Demian had really forgotten that story! It was so unpleasant to be under that obligation to him; it was actually just a stupid story of children's doings, but nevertheless, it was an obligation...

He seemed to wait and see whether I would greet him, and when I did so as casually as possible, he gave me his hand. That was his handshake again! So firm and warm, yet unemotional and manly!

He looked attentively at my face and said: "You've grown tall, Sinclair." He himself looked quite unchanged, just as old and just as young as always.

He joined me, we took a walk and spoke about unimportant things only, nothing about the old days. I recalled that at one time I had written to him more than once without receiving a reply. Oh, if only he had forgotten that as well, those stupid, stupid letters! He didn't mention them!

When this occurred there was still no Beatrice and no portrait, I was still in the midst of my dissolute period. At the edge of town, I invited him to go to a tavern with me. He went along. Boastfully I ordered a bottle of wine, poured, clinked glasses with him, and showed that I was quite familiar with students' drinking customs; in fact, I drained the first glass in one draft.

"Do you go to the tavern a lot?" he asked me.

"Oh, yes," I said lazily, "what else is one to do? When you come down to it, it's still the most entertaining thing."

"You think so? Maybe it is. Anyway, something about it is very fine—intoxication, the bacchic aspect of it! But I find that for most people who spend lots of time in taverns that's altogether lost. It seems to me as if frequenting taverns, especially, is something truly Philistine. Yes, for one night, with burning torches, working up to a real, beautiful frenzy and delirium! But to go on and on in the same way, one glass after another, that can't be true, can it? For instance, can you picture Faust sitting night after night at a table reserved for regulars?"

I drank and looked at him hostilely.

"Yes, but not everyone happens to be Faust," I said curtly.

He looked at me, somewhat puzzled.

Then he laughed with his old vigor and superiority.

"Well, why argue about it? At any rate, the life of a drunkard or libertine is presumably livelier than that of the faultless citizen. And then—I read it once—the life of libertine is one of the best preparations for becoming a mystic. It's always people like Saint Augustine who become seers. Earlier in life he, too, was an epicure and a playboy."

I was suspicious and didn't want him to lord it over me. So I said in my blasé manner: "Yes, everyone to his own taste! To be perfectly honest, I am totally unconcerned with becoming a seer or anything like that."

Demian's knowing eyes, slightly narrowed, flashed at me.

"My dear Sinclair," he said slowly, "it wasn't my intention to say anything unpleasant to you. Besides, the purpose for which you're now drinking your glasses of wine, neither I nor you know. The thing in you that constitutes your life, already knows why. It's so good to know this: that inside us there's a self that knows everything, wills everything, does everything better than we ourselves do.—But excuse me, I must get home."

Our leavetaking was brief. I kept sitting there, very much out of sorts, finished my bottle, and discovered, when about to leave, that Demian had already paid for it. That annoyed me even more.

My thoughts were once more centered on that minor incident. They were filled with Demian. And the words he had spoken in that suburban tavern resurfaced in my memory, oddly fresh and unforgettable. "It's so good to know that inside us there's a self that knows everything!"

I looked at the picture hanging in the window and now it is completely dark. But I saw the eyes still gleaming. That was Demian's gaze. Or else it was the self inside me. The one that knows everything.

How I missed Demian! I didn't know a thing about him, he was inaccessible to me. I only knew that presumably he was a student at some university and that, after he finished secondary school, his mother had moved away from our town.

Going all the way back to my relations with Kromer, I searched out every recollection of Max Demian. How many things that he had once said to me I now heard once again! And everything was still meaningful, timely, and of concern to me! Even what he had said at our last, very unpleasant meeting, about libertines and saints, was suddenly clearly present in my soul. Hadn't things gone with me in precisely that way? Hadn't I lived in drunkenness and dirt, numb and lost, until with a new impulse in life the exact opposite had come to life within me, the longing for purity, the yearning for sanctity?

Thus I continued to pursue my memories; night had fallen some time back, and outside it was raining. In my memories, too, I heard it raining; it was the time under the chestnut trees when he had once questioned me about Franz Kromer and had guessed my first secrets. One thing after another came to mind, conversations on the way to school, Confirmation lessons. And finally, I recalled my very first meeting with Max Demian. Now, what has it been about? I didn't hit on it right away, but I gave myself time, I was completely absorbed in the subject. And now I recall it, that also. We had been standing in front of my house, after he had let me know his opinion about Cain. Then he had spoken about the old, obliterated coat-of-arms located above our entryway, on that keystone which got broader from bottom to top. He had said he was interested in it, and that people should pay attention to such things.

That night I dreamt about Demian and the coat-of-arms. It kept changing shape, Demian was holding it in his hands, often it was small and gray, often terrifically big and multicolored, but he explained to me that it was nevertheless one and the same. But finally he persuaded me to eat the coat-of-arms. After I gulped it down, I felt with horrible fright that the bird in the coat-of-arms I had swallowed was alive inside me, was filling all the space there, and was beginning to consume me from within. Filled with deathly fear, I woke up with a start.

My mind cleared; it was the middle of the night, and I heard the rain coming into the room. I got up to shut the window and, as I did so, I stepped on a bright object that was lying on the floor. In the morning, I discovered that it was the picture I had painted. It was lying on the wet floor and had curled up. I spread it out between two sheets of blotting paper and pressed it inside a heavy book to dry. When I went to look at it the following day, it was dry. But it had changed. The red mouth had become paler and a little narrower. Now it was altogether Demian's mouth.

I now set about painting a new picture, the bird in the coat-of-arms. I no longer clearly remembered exactly what it looked like, and, as I knew, some of its details couldn't be made out even close up, because it was old and had frequently been painted over. The bird was standing or sitting on something, perhaps on a flower, or on a basket or nest, or on a treetop. I didn't worry about that, but began with the elements I had a clear idea of. Out of some obscure necessity I began at once with strong colors; the bird's head in my picture was golden yellow. As the mood took me, I continued working on it and finished it in a few days.

Now it was a bird of prey with the sharp, bold head of a sparrowhawk. The lower part of its body was enclosed in a dark terrestrial globe, from which it was working itself free, as if from a gigantic egg; the background was sky-blue. As I studied the picture longer, it seemed more and more to me as if it was the brightly colored coat-of-arms that had appeared in my dream.

I wouldn't have been able to write a letter to Demian even if I had known where to send it. But with that same dream-like presentiment that was guiding all my actions at the time, I decided to send him the picture of the sparrowhawk, whether it reached him or not. I wrote no message on it, not even my name; I trimmed the edges carefully, bought a large envelope, and wrote my friend's former address on it. Then I mailed it.

An exam was approaching, and I had to spend more time on schoolwork than usual. I had been back in the teachers' good graces ever since I suddenly changed my disgraceful ways. Even now I probably wasn't a good student, but neither I, nor anyone else still thought about the fact that six months earlier my punitive expulsion from school had been expected by everyone.

My father was now writing to me more in his former tone again, without reproaches or threats. But I felt no urge to explain to him or anyone else in what way the change in me had taken place. It was only an accident that this change coincided with the wishes of my parents and teachers. This change didn't bring me closer to others, or make me intimate with anyone, it only made me lonelier. It was directed at some goal, at Demian, at a far-off destiny. I didn't know what it was, for I was in the midst of it. It had begun with Beatrice, but for some time I had been living with my paintings and thoughts of Demian in such a totally unreal world that even she vanished completely from my sight and thoughts. I couldn't have said a word to anyone about my dreams, my expectations, my inner transformation, even if I had wanted to.

But how could I have wanted to?

CHAPTER 5

The Bird Fights its Way Out of the Egg

My painted dream-bird was on its way, seeking out my friend. I received a reply in the strangest way.

Once, in my classroom, at my seat, after the break between two lessons, I found a note sticking out of my book. It was folded exactly the way we usually did when classmates occasionally sent one another private messages during a lesson. The only thing I wondered about was who had sent me such a note, because I was never on such terms with any of my schoolmates. I thought it would be an invitation to join in some schoolboy prank, which I certainly wouldn't participate in, and I stuck the note into the front of my book without reading it. It was only during the lesson that it accidentally fell into my hands again.

I played with the paper, unfolded it without thinking about what I was doing, and found a few words written on it. I cast a glance at it, and my attention was caught by one word; I got frightened and read it, while my heart contracted in the face of destiny as if it had suffered a strong chill:

"The bird is fighting its way out of the egg. The egg is the world. Whoever wishes to be born must destroy a world. The bird is flying to God. The god is named Abraxas."

After reading those lines several times, I was plunged into deep reflection. Without a possible doubt, it was a reply from Demian. No one could know about the bird except the two of us. He had received my picture. He had understood it and was helping me to interpret it. But how was it all connected? And—this tormented me especially—what was the meaning of Abraxas? I had never heard or read the word. "The god is named Abraxas."

The lesson ended and I hadn't heard anything the teacher said. The next one began, the last for the morning. It was given by a young auxiliary teacher, fresh from the university; we liked him already because he was so young and didn't put on false airs of dignity with us.

Under Dr. Follen's direction, we were reading Herodotus. This reading was one of the few academic subjects that interested me. But this time I wasn't paying attention. I had opened my book mechanically, but I wasn't following along as the students translated; I was lost in my own thoughts. Besides, I had already found out several times how right Demian had been about what he had once told me in our religion class. If you wanted something hard enough, you succeeded. Whenever I was greatly occupied with my own thoughts during a class, I could be sure the teacher would let me alone. Yes, whenever you were distracted or sleepy, there he was all of a sudden: that, too, had already happened to me. But when you were really thinking, really concentrating, you were protected: 'And I had already tried out that business with hard starting, too, and had found that it worked. Back then in

Demian's time, I hadn't succeeded, but now I often observed that you could accomplish quite a lot by looking and thinking.

So now, too, I sat there, far away from Herodotus and school. But then unexpectedly the teacher's voice burst into my consciousness like a lightning flash, so I woke up in a panic. I heard his voice, he was standing right next to me, I thought he had called my name. But he wasn't looking at me. I was relieved.

Then I heard his voice again. Loudly it spoke the word: "Abraxas."

Dr. Follen continued an explanation of the beginning of which I had missed: "We mustn't imagine that the views of those sects and mystic associations of antiquity were as naïve as they seem from the standpoint of rationalistic examination. The ancients were altogether unacquainted with science in our sense of the word. Instead, they were concerned with philosophical and mystical truths to a highly developed degree. One result of this was magic and tomfoolery that, to be sure, frequently led to swindling and crime. But magic, too, had noble origins and profound thoughts. For example, the doctrine of Abraxas, which I cited earlier. Scholars speak that name in connection with Greek magical formulas, and many consider it to be the name of some devil associated with magic, such as primitive peoples still worship today. But it seems that Abraxas has a much greater significance. We may look upon the name as that of a deity who had the symbolic task of combining the godlike and the devilish."

The learned little man continued speaking elegantly and eagerly; no one paid much attention, and, since the name didn't occur again, my own attention was soon withdrawn into myself again.

"Combining the godlike and the devilish," resounded in my ears. This was something that touched me personally. It was familiar to me from my talks with Demian in the very last stage of our friendship. Demian had then said that we most likely had a God, whom we revered, but that He represented only an arbitrarily detached half of the world (this was the official, permissible, "bright" world). But we had to be able to revere the whole world, and so either we had to have a God who was also the Devil, or else we had to establish a service of the Devil alongside our divine service of God.—And now, then, Abraxas was the god who was both God and Devil.

For a time I pursued the trail further, but made no progress. I also leafed through an entire library looking for Abraxas, with no success. But my nature was never much inclined toward this sort of direct, conscious searching, in which at first you only find truths that lie in your hands like lifeless stones.

The figure of Beatrice, which for some time had occupied me so greatly and profoundly, now gradually submerged, or, rather, it moved slowly away from me, getting closer and closer to the horizon and becoming more shadowy, distant, and pallid. It was no longer enough for my soul.

Now, in that oddly self-centered existence that I was leading like a dreaming sleepwalker, a new development began to take shape. A longing for life blossomed with me—rather, the longing for love and my sexual drives, which for a time I had been able to sublimate in my adoration of Beatrice, were demanding new images and goals. No fulfillment was coming my way as yet, and I found it more impossible than ever to delude my longing and expect anything from the girls with whom my schoolmates were seeking their happiness. I was once more dreaming frequently, and more by day than at night. Ideas, images, or wishes rose up in my mind and drew me away from the world outside, so that I lived and conversed with these mental images, these dreams or shadows, more truly and vividly than with my real surroundings.

A certain dream, or play of imagination, that kept recurring became meaningful to me. This dream, the most important and memorable in my life, was more or less like this: I was returning to my father's house—over the doorway the bird in the coat-of-arms shone in yellow against a blue background—in the house my mother came up to me—but when I walked in and wanted to embrace her, it was no longer she but a figure I had never seen, tall and power, resembling Max Demian and my portrait painting, but different and, despite its mightiness, completely feminine. This figure drew me to itself and received me in a loving embrace that was profoundly thrilling. Rapture and horror were mingled, the embrace was a divine service but also a crime. There was too much lurking in the figure embracing me that was reminiscent of my mother, too much that was reminiscent of my friend Demian. Its embrace was a breach of all respect, and yet was blissful. I often awoke from that dream with a feeling of profound happiness, often with deathly fear, my conscience tortured as if by some frightful sin.

Only gradually and unconsciously was a connection established between that exclusively mental picture and the hint about the god I must seek that had come to me from outside. But then the connection became tighter and more intimate, and I began to notice that, in that very dream of premonition, I was invoking Abraxas. Rapture and terror, man and woman combined, the most sacred and the most hideous things interwoven, deep guilt quivering in the heart of the gentlest innocence—such was the image of my dream of love, and such was Abraxas, also. Love was no longer an obscure animal urge, as I had conceived it anxiously at the beginning, nor was it any longer a spiritualized pious worship, such as I had offered to the image of Beatrice. It was both, both and much more still, it was an angelic image and Satan, man and woman in one, human being and animal, the highest good and extreme evil. To experience this seemed to be my lot; to taste it, my destiny. I longed for it and feared it, but it was always there, always hovering over me.

The following spring I was to leave secondary school and go to a university, I didn't yet know where, or what I would study. A little moustache was growing above my lips, I was a grown man, and yet completely helpless and aimless. Only one thing was certain: the voice within me, the dream image. I felt it incumbent on me to follow that lead blindly. But it was hard for me, and I rebelled daily. "Maybe I'm crazy," I often thought; "maybe I'm not like other people." But I could do everything the others were capable of; with a little diligence and effort, I could read Plato, solve problems in trigonometry, or follow a chemical analysis. There was only one thing I couldn't do: tear out the obscurely hidden aim within me and visualize it somewhere before my eyes, as others did, those who knew precisely that they wanted to become a professor, judge, doctor, or artist, who knew how long that would take them and what benefits it would bring them. I couldn't do that. Maybe I would become something of the sort in the future, but how was I to know? Perhaps I might even have to seek and seek for years and never become anything or reach any goal. Perhaps I might reach some goal, but it would be evil, perilous, frightening.

All I really wanted was to try and live the life that was spontaneously welling up within me. Why was that so very difficult?

I often made the attempt to paint the powerful amorous figure of my dream. But I never succeeded. If I had succeeded,

I would have sent the picture to Demian. Where was he? I didn't know. I only knew that he was linked to me. When would I see him again?

The welcome repose I had enjoyed during the weeks and months of the Beatrice period was long past. At the time I had thought I had reached an island and found peace. But that's how it always went—as soon as one condition had become dear to me, as soon as a dream had comforted me, it was already withering and tarnished. No use lamenting over it. I was now living in a blaze of unsatisfied desire, of suspenseful expectancy, that often made me wild and crazy. I often saw the image of my dream beloved before me with more than lifelike clarity, much more clearly than my own hand; I spoke to it, wept before it, cursed it. I called it mother and knelt before it in tears; I called it beloved and sensed it's ripe, all-fulfilling kiss; I called it devil and whore, vampire and murderer. It lured me into the tenderest dreams of love and into acts of dissolute shamelessness; nothing was too good and precious for it, nothing too bad and vile.

I spent that whole winter in a mental storm that's hard for me to describe. I had been long accustomed to solitude, it didn't oppress me; I lived with Demian, with the sparrowhawk, with the image of the tall dream figure that was my destiny and my beloved. That was enough to live in, because it all looked toward great, distant things, and it all pointed toward Abraxas. But none of these dreams, none of these thoughts obeyed me; I couldn't summon any of them, I couldn't lend color to any of them at will. They came and took me over; I was governed by them, they lived my life.

To be sure, I was outwardly secured. I had no fear of people; my schoolmates had found that out, too, and showed me secret respect that often made me smile. Whenever I wished, I could see through most of them very well and occasionally amaze them that way. But I seldom or never felt like it. I was always occupied with myself, always. And I desired ardently to experience a bit of life finally, to give something of myself to the world, to create a relationship with it and do battle with it. Sometimes, when I roamed through the streets in the evening and, in my restlessness, was unable to return to my room until midnight, I would imagine that I just must meet my beloved now; she would pass by at the next corner, call me from the nearest window. Sometimes, too, all this seemed unbearably painful to me, and I was mentally prepared to take my life at some point.

At that time I found a peculiar refuge—by "accident," as people say. But there are no such accidents. When someone who badly needs something finds it, it isn't an accident that brings it his way, but he, his own desire and necessity lead him to it.

Two or three times on my walks through town, I had heard organ music coming from a smallish suburban church, but I had never stopped to listen. When I passed by the next time, I heard it again and recognized the music as being by Bach. I went to the door, which I found locked, and since there was practically no one in the street, I sat down next to the church on a curbstone, pulled my coat collar up around my neck, and listened. It wasn't a big organ but a good one, and it was being played marvelously, with a unique, highly personal expressiveness, filled with willpower and perseverance, that sounded like a prayer. I felt that the man playing there knew that a treasure was locked away in that music, and was suing, insisting, and striving for that treasure as if for his life. In the technical sense, I don't understand very much about music, but ever since my childhood, I have instinctively understood precisely this soulful expressiveness, and I have felt musicality as something natural inside me.

After that the musician played something modern, too, perhaps by Reger. The church was almost completely dark, with just a very thin ray of light coming in from the nearest window. I waited until the music was over, and then prowled up and down until I saw the organist coming out. He was still young, though older than me, with a burly, squat figure, and he walked away rapidly with strong and seemingly reluctant steps.

From that time on, at the evening hour, I frequently sat or paced back and forth in front of the church. Once I found the door open and sat in a pew for half an hour, feeling cold but happy, while the organist was playing above by the meager gaslight. In the music he played, I didn't merely hear him himself. In addition to that, everything he played seemed to me to be interrelated, with some secret connection. Everything he played was religious, devout, and pious, but not with the piety of churchgoers and pastors—rather, with the piety of medieval pilgrims and beggars; it was pious with an unconditional surrender to a universal emotion that rose above any particular faith. He diligently played composers earlier than Bach, and old Italian masters. And they all stated the same thing, they all stated what the musician had in his soul as well: longing, the most intimate grasping of the world and the most reckless separation from it again, an ardent listening to one's own obscure soul, a frenzy of devotion and a profound curiosity for the miraculous.

Once, as I was secretly following the organist after he left the church, I saw him enter a small tavern far out at the edge of town. I couldn't resist, and I followed him in. Here for the first time, I had a clear look at him. He was sitting at a table in one corner of the small room, his black felt hat on his head, a glass of wine in front of him, and his face was just as I had expected. It was ugly and rather wild, the face of a seeker, stubborn, mulish, and strong-willed, but at the same time soft and childlike around the mouth. All his masculinity and strength were in the eyes and forehead, while the lower part of his face was tender and immature, uncontrolled and somewhat weak; his chin, full of indecisiveness, was like a boy's, in contrast to his forehead and eyes. I liked his dark brown eyes, filled with pride and hostility.

I sat down opposite him in silence; there was no one else in the tavern. He glared at me as if he wanted to chase me away. But I kept my ground and looked at him steadily until he rudely grumbled: "Why are you staring so damn hard? Do you want something from me?"

"I don't want anything from you," I said. "But I've already received a lot from you."

He furrowed his brow.

"So you're a music fan? I find it disgusting to be a music fan."

I didn't let myself be scared away.

"I've already listened to you often, in the church down there," I said. "Anyhow, I don't want to bother you. I thought I might find something in you, something special, I don't rightly know what. But it's better if you don't listen to me! After all, I can listen to you in church."

"But I always lock the door."

"Recently you forgot to, and I sat inside. Usually I stand outside or sit on the curbstone."

"Is that right? Next time you can come in, it's warmer. All you need to do is knock at the door. But hard, and not while I'm playing. Now; out with it—what did you want to say? You're a very young man, probably a secondary-school or university student. Are you a musician?"

"No. I like listening to music, but only the kind you play, absolute music, the kind that makes you feel that someone is rattling at the doors of heaven and hell. I like music very much, I think, because it's so unconcerned with morality. Everything else is moralistic, and I'm looking for something that isn't. I've always derived nothing but suffering from morality. I can't express it properly. Do you know that there must be a God who is both God and the Devil? They say there once was one, I've heard about it."

The musician pushed his broad hat back a little and shook the dark hair away from his large forehead. While doing so, he gave me a penetrating look and bent his face toward me over the table.

In a quiet, tense voice he asked: "What's the name of the god you're talking about?"

"Unfortunately I know almost nothing about him, actually only his name, which is Abraxas."

The musician looked around, as if suspiciously, as if someone could be spying on us. Then he moved close to me and whispered: "I thought as much. Who are you?"

"I'm a secondary-school student."

"How did you find out about Abraxas?"

"By accident."

He banged on the table, making his wineglass run over.

"Accident! Don't talk crap,[6] young men! No one hears about Abraxas by accident, make a note of that! I'll tell you even more about him. I know a little about him."

He fell silent and pushed his chair back. When I looked at him with vivid expectations, he grimaced.

"Not here! Another time.—Take this!"

---

6. The word scheiβdreck was abbreviated in the German text.

As he said this, he reached into the pocket of his coat, which he hadn't taken off, and pulled out a few roasted chestnuts, which he tossed in front of me.

I said nothing, took them, ate them, and was very content.

"So, then!" he whispered after a pause. "Where did you hear about—him?"

I didn't hesitate to tell him.

"I was alone and at a loss," I recounted. "Then I recalled a friend of earlier days, who I believe knows a great deal. I had painted a picture, a bird emerging from a globe. I sent it to him. After a while, when I didn't really expect it anymore, I found a piece of paper in my hand which was written: 'The bird is fighting its way out of the egg. The egg is the world. Whoever wishes to be born must destroy a world. The bird is flying to God. The god is named Abraxas.'"

He made no response; we peeled our chestnuts and ate them with the wine.

"Shall we have another glass?" he asked.

"No, thanks. I don't like to drink."

He laughed, somewhat disappointed.

"As you like! It's different for me. I'm going to stay here longer. You can go now!"

The next time I went with him after his organ session, he wasn't very communicative. He led me to a narrow old street and up through an imposing old house into a large, rather gloomy and squalid room, in which only the piano gave any hint of music, whereas a tall bookcase and desk gave the room the air of a scholar's study.

"You've got a lot of books!" I said admiringly.

"Part of it is from my father's library; I live with him.—Yes, young man, I live with my father and mother, but I can't introduce you to them; the company I keep isn't well thought of in this house. You see, I'm a prodigal son. My father is a fabulously respectable man, an eminent person and preacher in this town. And I, to inform you right away, am his talented and promising son, who, however, has gone wrong and is a little crazy. I was a divinity student, but shortly before the government examination, I abandoned that honorable faculty. Though I'm actually still in the same department, as far as my private studies are concerned. I'm still interested and fascinated by the sorts of gods that people have invented for themselves in the course of history. Besides that, I'm now a musician, and it seems that I'll soon get a small post as an organist. Then I'll be associated with the Church again."

I looked at the spines of the books and discovered titles in Greek, Latin, and Hebrew, as far as I could tell by the feeble light of the small table lamp. Meanwhile, my new acquaintance had lain down on the floor near the wall in the dark and was doing something there.

"Come," he called after a while, "let's practice a little philosophy now; that is, let's shut up, lie on our stomachs, and think."

He lit a match and set fire to papers and logs in the fireplace in front of which he was lying. The flame shot up high; he poked and fed the fire with extreme care. I lay down beside him on the worn-out carpet. He stared into the fire, which attracted me, too, and we lay on our stomachs in silence for about an hour in front of the flickering wood fire, watching it flame and roar, collapse and curl, flicker away in spurts, and finally brood on the fireplace floor as a quiet, sunken glow.

"Fire worship wasn't the dumbest thing ever invented," he murmured to himself at one point. Aside from that, neither of us said a word. With rigid eyes I stared at the fire as I sank into dreams and silence, seeing forms in the smoke and images in the ashes. At one point I became alarmed. My companion threw a small piece of resin into the fire; a small, narrow flame shot up, in which I saw the bird with the yellow sparrowhawk's head. In the dying glow of the fireplace, gold-gleaming threads were combining into nets, letters of the alphabet and images were appearing, reminiscences of faces, animals, plants, worms, and snakes. When I awoke and looked at the other man, he was resting his chin on his two fists and staring devotedly and fanatically at the ashes...

"I must go now," I said quietly.

"All right, go. Till next time!"

He didn't get up, and since the lamp was out, I had to grope my way painfully through the darkroom and the dark corridors and stairs and out of the old enchanted house. In the street, I halted and looked up at the old house. There was no light in any window. A small brass sign gleamed in the light from the gaslamp in front of the door.

"Pïstorius, Head Pastor," I read.

It was only when back home, sitting alone after supper in my small room, that I realized that I had learned nothing either about Abraxas or Pistorius, that we had barely exchanged ten words altogether. But I was very content with my visit to him. And he had promised that next time he would play a truly exquisite piece of old organ music, a passacaglia by Buxtehude.

Without my knowing it, the organist Pistorius had given me an introductory lesson when I lay beside him before the fireplace on the floor of his dreary hermit's room. Looking into the fire had done me good; it had strengthened and confirmed inclinations that

I had always possessed, but had never really cultivated. Gradually I came to recognize them to some extent.

Even as a small child I had occasionally had a leaning toward looking at bizarre natural forms, not as an observer, but surrendering myself to their unique magic, their confused but profound language. Long, woody tree roots, veins of color in stones, patches of oil floating on water, cracks in glass—all such things had occasionally cast a strong spell over me, especially water and fire, as well, smoke, clouds, dust, and most particularly the moving dots of color I saw when I shut my eyes. In the days after my first visit to Pistorius, this began to occur to me again. Because I noticed that a certain strengthening and joy, a heightening of my perception of self, which I had perceived ever since then, was due solely to my long staring into the open fire. It was oddly pleasurable and enriching to do that!

To the few things I had learned so far on the way to my true aim in life, this new thing was now added: The contemplation of such shapes, the surrender to irrational, confused, rare natural forms, engenders in us a feeling that our own mind is in harmony with the will that gave rise to these forms—we soon feel the temptation to look on them as our own caprices, as our own creations—we see the borderline between us and nature tremble and dissolve, and we become acquainted with the mood in which we don't know whether the images on our retina are coming from external impressions or from within us. In no other way than through this practice do we discover so simply and easily how very creative we are, how much our soul always participates in the perpetual creation of the world. Rather, it's the same indivisible godhead that is active in us and in nature; and if the outside world were to perish, anyone of us would be capable of reconstructing it, because mountain and river, tree and leaf, root and blossom, every form in nature, has a pre-image inside us; it originates from the soul, whose nature is eternity, whose nature we don't know but is generally revealed to us as the power of love and creativity.

Only many years later did I find this observation confirmed in a book, namely in Leonardo da Vinci, who says in one place how good and deeply stimulating it is to look at a wall on which many people have a spat. Seeing those stains on the damp wall, he had the same feelings Pistorius and I had in front of the fire.

At our next meeting, the organist gave me an explanation.

"We always limit our personality much too narrowly! We always count as pertaining to our person only what we recognize as individual differences that set us apart. But we're composed of everything that comprises the world, each of us, and just as our body bears within it the lines of evolutionary descent all the way back to the fish and even much farther beyond that, in the same way, our soul contains everything that has ever dwelt in human souls. All the gods and devils that ever existed, whether among the Greeks, Chinese, or Zulus, are all inside us, they exist there as possibilities, as wishes, as ways of escape. If mankind died out except for a single halfway-gifted child that had received no education, that child would rediscover the whole course of events, it would be able to produce against the gods, demons, Edens, positive and negative commandments, the Old and the New Testament."

"Fine," I objected; "but what then comprises the worth of the individual? Why do we still strive for things when everything is already there within us?"

"Stop right there!" Pistorius shouted. "There's a big difference between merely carrying the world inside you and knowing that you do! A madman can produce ideas that resemble Plato's, and a pious little schoolboy in a Herrnhut institute[7] can creatively reconstruct profound mythological associations in his mind, ideas to be found in the Gnostics or Zoroaster. But he doesn't know he's doing it! He's a tree or a stone, at best an animal, just as long as he doesn't know that. But when the first spark of that knowledge glimmers, he becomes a human being. You certainly don't consider all the bipeds running around the street to be human beings merely because they walk upright and carry their young for nine months? After all, you see how many of them are fish or sheep, worms or leeches, how many are ants, how many are bees! Now, each one of them has the potential of becoming a human being, but only when he senses that potential, when he even learns to be conscious of it to some degree, does that potential belong to him."

Our conversations were more or less of that type. They seldom offered me anything completely new or totally surprising. But all of them, even the most banal, hit the same spot in me with a steady, gentle hammer blow; they all helped form my character, they all helped to strip dead skins off me, to crush eggshells; and after each one, I raised my head a little higher, a little more freely, until my yellow bird pushed its beautiful predator's head out of the shattered globe.

Often we told each other our dreams. Pistorius knew how to interpret them. Right now I can remember a marvelous example. I had a dream in which I was able to fly, but in such a way that to some degree I was catapulted through the air by some mighty impetus that I couldn't control. The sensation of that flight was uplifting, but soon turned to fear when I found myself hurled into dangerous heights involuntarily. Then I made the relieving

7. The Hermit church, an unaligned Protestant denomination founded in the 18th century, is associated with the Pietism prevalent in that era.

discovery that I could regulate my rise and fall by holding my breath and releasing it again.

When I told him that, Pistorius said: "The impetus that makes you fly is the great store of humanity that each of us possesses. It's the feeling of interconnectedness with the roots of all power, but we soon get alarmed by it! It's damned dangerous! And so most people are glad to give up flying; they prefer walking on the sidewalk, following the rules and regulations. But not you. You keep on flying, as a clever fellow should. And, look, as you do so, you discover the marvelous fact that you gradually become a master of it, that in addition to the great general power that bears you aloft, subtle, small power of your own is added, an internal organ, a rudder! That's terrific. Without, it we'd be wafted away into the sky involuntarily, as madmen are, for example. They are endowed with deeper presentiments than the people on the sidewalk, but they have no key to it and no rudder, and they whiz away into the abyss. But you, Sinclair, you can pull it off. And how, I ask? I suppose you don't know yet. You do it by using a new organ, a breath regulator. And now you can see that your soul, deep down, isn't all that 'personal.' Because you didn't invent that regulator! It's not new! It's a loan, it has existed for millennia. It's the organ of equilibrium that fish have, the air bladder. And in fact, there are still a few rare, conservative species of fish extant today in which the air bladder is also a kind of lung and under certain conditions can actually be used for breathing. So they're precisely like the lungs you use as a flying bladder in your dream!"

He even brought me a zoology book and showed me the names and pictures of those primitive fish. And with a peculiar thrill, I felt that a function from early evolutionary stages was alive in me.

CHAPTER 6

JACOB'S FIGHT WITH THE ANGEL

What I learned about Abraxas from the eccentric musician Pistorius I cannot relate briefly. But the most important thing I learned from him was a further step on the path to myself. Around eighteen at the time, I was an unusual young person, precocious in a hundred ways but very undeveloped and helpless in a hundred others. When I had occasionally compared myself with others, I had often been proud and smug, but just as often depressed and humiliated. I had often thought of myself as a genius, often as half-crazy. I couldn't manage to share in the joys and activities of those my age, and I had often been consumed with self-reproaches and worries, as if I were hopelessly cut off from them, as if I were shut off from life.

Pistorius, who was a full-fledged eccentric himself, taught me to keep up my courage and self-respect. By constantly finding something of value in my words, dreams, fantasies, and ideas, by constantly taking them seriously and discussing them earnestly, he set me an example.

"You told me," he said, "that you love music because it's not moralistic. All right. But you mustn't be a moralist, either! You shouldn't compare yourself with others; and if nature has made you a bat, you shouldn't try to turn yourself into an ostrich. You sometimes think you're peculiar, you reproach yourself for going other ways than most people. You've got to get that out of your head. Look into the fire, look into the clouds, and as soon as your presentiments come and the voices in your soul begin to speak, surrender yourself to them and don't start off by asking whether that suits or pleases your teacher, your father, or some God or other! If you do that, you'll ruin yourself. That way you get on the sidewalk and you become a fossil. My friend Sinclair, our god is named Abraxas; he is God and Satan; both the bright world and the dark world are contained in him. Abraxas has no objections to any of your thoughts or any of your dreams. Never forget that. But he'll abandon you if you ever become faultless and normal. Then he'll abandon you and look for a new pot to cook his ideas in."

Among all my dreams, that obscure dream of love was the most loyal. I dreamt it over and over again; I walked beneath the heraldic bird into our old house, I wanted to draw my mother to my bosom and, in her place, I embraced that tall woman who was half-masculine and half-maternal; I was afraid of her and yet I was drawn to her by the most burning desire. And I could never tell my friend that dream. I held it back after revealing everything else to him. It was my cranny, my secret, my refuge.

Whenever I was downcast I asked Pistorius to play that passacaglia by the old master Buxtehude. Then I sat in the dark church in the evening, lost in that strange, intimate music which seemed to be submerged in itself, to be listening to itself;

each time it soothed me and left me better prepared to acknowledge the voices in my soul.

Sometimes we remained seated in the church for a while after the organ tones had already died away, and we saw the dim light shine through the tall Gothic arches of the windows and become lost in the darkness.

"It sounds funny;" Pistorius said, "that I once was a divinity student and almost became a person. But the error I then made was merely one of form. To be a priest is my vocation and my goal. But I became satisfied too soon, placing myself at Jehovah's disposal even before I knew Abraxas. Ah, every religion is beautiful. Religion is the soul, whether you take Communion as a Christian or you make a pilgrimage to Mecca."

"In that case," I said, "you might just as well have become a person."

"No, Sinclair, no. I would have had to lie. Our religion is practiced as if it weren't one. It behaves as if it were entirely rational. In a pinch, I could be a Catholic, but a Protestant clergyman—no! The handful of true believers—I know some—abide by the literal meaning; I couldn't tell them, for example, that for me Christ is not an individual, but a hero, a myth, an enormous shadow in which mankind sees its own image cast onto the wall of eternity. And the rest, those who come to church to hear a wise saying, to fulfill a duty, to avoid being negligent, and so on, what was I supposed to tell them? Was I to convert them, you think? But I don't want to! A priest isn't out for conversions, he wants to live only among believers, people like himself; he wants to be the bearer and the spokesman of the emotion out of which we create our gods."

He broke off. Then he continued: "Our new faith, for which we now choose Abraxas's name, is beautiful, my friend. It's the best thing we have. But it's still in its infancy! Its wings haven't grown yet. Ah, a solitary religion is not yet true. It has to become the religion of the community, it must have rites and frenzy, festivals and mysteries..."

He sank into meditation.

"Can't mysteries also be celebrated by one person or a very small circle?" I asked hesitantly.

"Yes, they can," he said, nodding his head. "I've been celebrating them for some time. I have performed rites for which I'd have to go to prison for years if people knew about them. But I know it's still not the real thing."

Suddenly he slapped me on the shoulder, making me start. "My boy," he said forcefully, "you, too, have mysteries. I know you must have dreams you don't tell me about. I don't want to know them. But I tell you: live out those dreams, play out your role in them, build altars to them! That still won't be perfect, but it's a way. It remains to be seen whether we, you and I and a few others, will renew the world. But within ourselves we must renew it daily, otherwise we're meaningless. Think it over! You're eighteen years old, Sinclair, you don't chase after streetwalkers, you must have dreams of love, wishes for love. Perhaps they're of such a kind that you're afraid of them. Don't be afraid! They're the best thing you have! You can believe me. I lost a lot by doing violence to my dreams of love when I was your age. No one should do that. If a person knows about Abraxas, he must no longer do that. He should be afraid of nothing and consider nothing taboo that the soul within us desires."

I was frightened and objected: "But a person can't just do everything that comes into his head! For instance, you mustn't kill someone because you can't stand him."

He moved closer to me.

"Under certain circumstances, you can do even that. Only, it's usually a mistake. And I don't mean you should simply do anything that comes to mind. No, but those ideas, which make some good sense, shouldn't be made harmful by chasing them away and moralizing about them. Instead of crucifying yourself or anyone else, you can drink wine from a chalice with solemn thoughts and conceive of that as the mystery of sacrifice while you're doing it. Even without such formal proceedings, you can treat your urges and so-called evil temptations with respect and love. Then they show their true sense, and they all make sense.—Whenever you next get some really wild or sinful idea, Sinclair, when you feel like killing someone or committing some terrifically obscene act, then remember for a moment that it's Abraxas who is imagining that in your mind! The person you'd like to kill is never Mr. So-and-so, he's definitely just a disguise. When we hate a person, what we hate in his image is something inside ourselves. Whatever isn't inside us can't excite us."

Pistorius had never told me anything that affected me so deeply in my inmost recesses. I was unable to reply. But the thing that had touched me most powerfully and oddly was the resemblance between that exhortation and speeches by Demian which had stayed with me for years and years. They didn't know about each other, yet they were both telling me the same thing.

"The things we see," Pistorius said quietly, "are the same things that are in us. The only reality is the one we have in us. That's why most people's lives are so unreal, because they consider the external images to be real and don't allow their own world within themselves to tell them anything. They can be happy that way. But when a person once knows the other way, he is no longer free to choose the path that most people follow. Sinclair, the path of the majority is easy, ours is hard. Let's go."

A few days later, after I had waited for him in vain twice, I came across him in the street late one evening, blowing around a comer in the cold night wind, alone, stumbling and besotted with a drink. I didn't want to call him. He walked past me without seeing me; he was staring straight ahead with burning, lonely eyes, as if following an obscure call from the unknown. I followed him for the length of a street; he drifted along as if pulled by an invisible string, his pace fanatical but weak and confused, like a ghost. Sadly I returned home, back to my unfulfilled dreams.

"That's how he's renewing the world in himself!" I thought, and yet at the same moment, I felt that it was a cheap, moralistic thought. What did I know of his dreams? Perhaps in his intoxication, he was treading a surer path than I was in my anxiety.

In the breaks between lessons, I had sometimes become aware that a classmate, to whom I had never paid attention, was trying to approach me. He was a short, weak-looking, skinny boy with thin, reddish-blonde hair, with something all his own in his gaze and his behavior. One evening as I arrived home, he was waiting in the street for me; he let me pass by him, then ran after me and stopped in front of my door.

"Do you want something from me?" I asked.

"I just want to talk with you," he said timidly. "Please walk a bit with me."

I followed him and noticed that he was extremely agitated and filled with expectancy. His hands were trembling.

"Are you a spiritualist?" he suddenly asked.

"No, Knauer," I said with a laugh. "No way. What put that in your head?"

"But you are a theosophist?"

"Again, no."

"Oh, don't be so secretive! I can tell very well there's something special about you. It's in your eyes. I firmly believe you consort with spirits. I'm not asking out of idle curiosity, Sinclair, oh no! I am a seeker, you know, and I'm so alone."

"Out with it!" I said encouragingly. "I don't know anything about spirits, of course; I live in my dreams, and that's what caught your attention. The other people live in dreams, too, but not on their own, that's the difference."

"Yes, maybe so," he whispered. "But what counts is the kind of dreams a person is living in.—Have you ever heard of white magic?"

I had to say no.

"It's when you learn to control your own powers. You can become immortal and also cast spells. Haven't you ever indulged in such practices?"

When I asked with curiosity what those practices were, he acted mysteriously at first, until I turned to go; then he came out with it.

"For example, if I want to fall asleep or concentrate, I do the following exercise: I think of something, for example, a word or a name, or a geometric figure. I impress it into my mind as hard as I can, I try to picture it in my head until I feel it's in there. Then I imagine it going down to my neck, and so on, until I'm entirely filled with it. Then I'm completely firm, and nothing can disturb my repose anymore."

I grasped his meaning to a degree. But I felt that he still had something else on his mind; he was oddly excited and hasty. I tried to make it easy for him to question me, and before long he revealed what he was really after.

"You practice continence, too, don't you?" he asked me anxiously.

"What do you mean? You mean, sexually?"

"Yes, yes. For two years I've been continental, ever since learning about the doctrine. Before that I used to commit a vice, you know which one.—And so, you've never been with a woman?"

"No," I said. "I've never found the right one."

"But if you did find the one you thought was right, would you sleep with her?"

"Yes, naturally.—If she had no objection," I said, a little sarcastically.

"Oh, then you're on the wrong path! You can only develop your inner powers if you remain perfectly on the continent. I've done it for two years. Two years and a little over a month! It's so hard! Sometimes I can barely stand it any longer."

"Listen, Knauer, I don't believe continence is so all-important."

"I know," he said defensively, "that's what everyone says. But I didn't expect it from you. Whoever wants to travel the higher mental path must remain pure, absolutely!"

"Well, do it! But I don't understand why someone is more 'pure,' when he suppresses his sex urges, than anyone else is. Or are you able to eliminate sex from all your thoughts and dreams as well?"

He looked at me in despair.

"No, that's just it! My God, and I have to! At night I have dreams that I can't even repeat to myself! Terrible dreams, you hear?"

I recalled what Pistorius had told me. But correct as I found his words to be, I couldn't pass them along, I couldn't give advice that didn't stem from my own experience, advice I did not yet feel myself capable of following. I became taciturn and felt humiliated because someone was seeking advice from me and I had none to give.

"I've tried everything!" Knauer was lamenting, as he stood there beside me. "I've done all that can be done, with cold water, with snow, with gymnastics and running, but nothing helps. Every night I wake up from dreams that are unthinkable. And the horrible thing is: when that happens, I gradually lose everything I learned mentally. By now I can barely manage to concentrate or put myself to sleep; often I lie awake all night long. I won't be able to go on like this much longer. If I finally can't fight the battle to the end, if I give in and make myself impure again, then I'm worse than all the rest, those who never fought at all. You understand that, don't you?"

I nodded, but couldn't add any words. He was beginning to bore me, and I got frightened at myself, seeing that his obvious distress and despair made no stronger impression on me. All I felt was: I can't help you.

"So there's nothing you can tell me?" he finally said, exhausted and sad. "Nothing at all? There just has to be a way! How do you manage it?"

"I can't tell you anything, Knauer. In such matters, people can't help each other. No one helped me, either. You have to meditate on your own needs, and then you must do whatever is in accord with your own real nature. Nothing else will help. If you can't find yourself, you won't find any spirits, either; that's what I think."

Disappointed and suddenly struck dumb, the little fellow looked at me. Then a sudden malice blazed up in his eyes, he made a face at me, and yelled furiously: "Oh, you're a fine saint, aren't you? You've got your vice, too, I know! You act like a philosopher, but secretly you're hung up on the same filth that I am, and everybody is! You're a pig, a pig, just like me. We're all pigs!"

I went away and left him standing there. He took two or three paces after me, then he hung back, turned around, and ran away. I was sick with a feeling of sympathy and revulsion, and I couldn't get rid of that feeling until I was back in my little room and had arranged my handful of pictures around me, surrendering to my own dreams with the most ardent warmth. Then my dream immediately recurred, about my doorway and its coat-of-arms, about my mother and the woman I didn't know; and I saw the woman's features with such surreal clarity that on that very evening I began to draw her picture.

When that drawing was finished, a few days later, traced onto the paper in dreamlike fifteen-minute stints as if unconsciously, I hung it up on my wall in the evening, moved my reading lamp in front of it, and stood before it as if facing a spirit with whom I had to fight until a decision was reached. It was a face resembling the earlier one, resembling my friend Demian, but in some features resembling me, as well. One eye was noticeably higher than the other; the direction of their gaze passed over and beyond me, in the rigidity of concentration, filled with destiny.

I stood before it and turned cold to the heart from inner exertion. I questioned the picture, I made accusations against it, I caressed it, I prayed to it; I called it mother, I called it beloved, I called it whore and trollop, I called it Abraxas. Meanwhile, things that Pistorius—or was it Demian?—had told me came to mind; I couldn't recall when they had been said, but I thought I was hearing them again. They concerned Jacob's fight with the angel of God, and Jacob's words: "I will not let you go unless you bless me."

The painted face in the lamplight changed each time I invoked it. It became bright and radiant, it became dark and gloomy; its pallid eye-lids fell, covering glazed eyes, or opened again, while the eyes flashed and gleamed; it was a woman, a man, a girl, a little child, an animal; it dissolved into a blot, then grew large and clear again. Finally, obeying a strong inner call, I closed my eyes and now saw the image inside me, stronger and more powerful. I wanted to kneel down before it, but it was so firmly inside me that I could no longer separate it from myself, as if it had become my pure ego.

Then I heard a heavy, muffled roar, like that of a spring storm, and I trembled with an indescribably new feeling of anxiety and experience. Stars flared up and went out before my eyes; memories reaching back to my earliest, most completely forgotten childhood, and even back to prior existences and early stages of evolution, flowed past me in throngs. But the memories, which seemed to be repeating my whole life and penetrating its deepest secrets, didn't stop at yesterday and today; they went farther, mirroring the future, tearing me away from today and into new life forms, whose images were bright and dazzling, but none of which I was later able to recall clearly.

During the night I awoke from a deep sleep; I was dressed, stretched out across the bed. I turned on the light, with the feeling that I must remember something important; I recalled nothing of the previous hours. I turned on the light, and my memory came back gradually. I looked for the picture; it was no longer hanging on the wall, but wasn't on the table, either. Then I thought I could dimly recall having burnt it. Or had I merely dreamt about burning it while holding it, and then eating the ashes?

I was driven by a great, pulsating unrest. I put on my hat, walked through the house onto the street, as if by compulsion; I walked on and on through streets and across squares as if blown onward by a storm; stopped to listen in front of my friend's church, now dark; sought and sought, not knowing what, in the obscurity of my impulse. I walked through a suburb of Bordellos, where some lights were still burning here and there. Further out, there were construction sites and piles of bricks, partially covered with gray snow. As I drifted through that wilderness like a sleepwalker propelled by an unknown force, I recalled the construction site in my hometown into which my tormentor Kromer had once pulled me for our first settlement of accounts. A similar site was located here in front of me on a gray night; the blackness of its empty doorway gaped at me. I felt drawn inside; I wanted to resist and I stumbled over sand and rubbish; the urge was stronger, I had to go in.

Over boards and shattered bricks, I reeled into the deserted space, which had a dismal smell of damp cold and stones. A heap of sand there formed a patch of light gray; aside from that, everything was dark.

Then a horrified voice called to me: "For God's sake, Sinclair, where did you come from?"

And beside me, a person loomed out of the darkness, a short, thin young fellow, like a spirit, and while my hair was still standing on end, I recognized my classmate Knauer.

"How did you get here?" he asked, as if mad with excitement. "How could you find me?"

I didn't understand.

"I wasn't looking for you," I said, stupefied; every word was an effort for me, painfully passing my dead, heavy, seemingly frozen lips.

He stared at me.

"Weren't you looking?"

"No. I felt drawn here. Did you call me? You must have called me. What are you doing here? It's the middle of the night!"

He convulsively threw his skinny arms around me.

"Yes, night. Morning must be coming soon. Oh, Sinclair, you didn't forget me! Can you forgive me?"

"For what?"

"Oh, I was so hateful, you know!"

It was only then that I remembered our conversation. Had that been four or five days earlier? I felt as if a lifetime had gone by since then. But now I suddenly knew everything. Not only what had passed between us, but also why I had come there and what Knauer had intended to do out there.

"So you wanted to take your life, Knauer?"

He shivered with cold and fear.

"Yes, I did: I don't know whether I could have done it. I wanted to wait until morning."

I led him out into the open. The first horizontal rays of daylight were shining, indescribably cold and listless, in the gray sky.

I led the boy by the arm for a stretch. A voice came from me, saying: "Now you're going home and you won't say a thing to anyone! You've been following the wrong path, the wrong path! And we're not pigs, as you think. We're human beings. We create gods and fight with them, and they bless us."

We continued walking in silence, then separated. When I got home it was daylight.

The best thing those days in St— still had in store for me was the hours I spent with Pistorius at the organ or in front of the fireplace.

Together we read a Greek text about Abraxas; he read aloud to me portions of a translation of the Vedas and taught me how to pronounce the sacred syllable om. Yet it wasn't these scholarly accomplishments that fostered my inner life; rather, it was just the opposite. What benefited me was my further progress in finding myself, my increasing confidence in my own dreams, ideas, and presentiments, and my increasing knowledge of the power I carried inside me.

I got along with Pistorius in every way. All I needed was to think about him hard, and I could be sure of a visit or a message from him. Just as the case had been with Demian, I could ask him something even if he wasn't present: I just had to imagine him clearly and address my questions to him in the form of intensive thoughts. Then all the psychic force I had expended on the question flowed back to me as the reply. Only, it wasn't the person of Pistorius that I imagined, or that of Max Demian; it was the picture I had dreamed and painted, the androgynous dream image of my daemon that I had to invoke. Now it no longer lived merely in my dreams or painted on paper, but inside me, as an ideal and a heightening of myself.

The relationship I had now formed with the failed suicide Knauer was peculiar and sometimes funny. Since that night in which I had been sent to him, he was devoted to me like a loyal servant or a dog; he tried to link his life to mine and he followed me blindly. He came to me with the oddest questions and wishes; he wanted to see spirits and learn Kabbalah, and he didn't believe me when I assured him that I knew nothing of all those matters. He thought I possessed every kind of power. But the strange thing was that often he came to me with his odd, stupid questions precisely when there was a knot in me that had to be untied, and his whimsical notions and requests often supplied me with the clue and the impetus for untying the knot. Often I lost patience with him and dismissed him imperiously, but I nevertheless perceived this: he, too, was sent to me; even from him I got back twofold everything I gave him; he, too, was a guide for me or, rather, a path. The crazy books and articles which he brought me, and in which he was seeking his salvation, taught me more than I could discern at the moment.

Later on, this Knauer disappeared from my path without me being aware of it. A decisive confrontation with him wasn't necessary. But, with Pistorius, it was. Toward the end of my school days in St— I had another peculiar experience with that friend.

Even innocuous people are hardly spared from coming into conflict, one time or more in their life, with the lovely virtues of piety and gratitude. Everyone must at some time take the step that separates him from his father, from his teachers; everyone must taste a little of the toughness of solitude, even though most people can't stand much of it and soon knuckle under again.—I hadn't parted from my parents and their world, the "bright" world of my beautiful childhood, in a violent battle, but I had grown more distant from them and more of a stranger to them slowly and almost imperceptibly. I was sorry about it; when I visited them back home, it often created bitter hours for me; but it didn't affect me in my vitals, it was bearable.

But in situations where we have made the gift of our love and veneration, not out of long familiarity but out of our most personal impulses; where we have been disciples and friends from the depth of our heart—in such cases it's a bitter and frightening moment when we suddenly seem to realize that the principal current within us is determined to carry us away from the person we love. Then every thought that rejects our friend and teacher turns its poisoned barb against our own bosom; then each defensive blow we strike hits our own face. Then anyone who imagined he was harboring a valid morality in his heart, feels the words "disloyalty" and "ingratitude" looming up like catcalls and stigmas; then one's frightened heart flees fearfully back to the cherished valleys of childhood virtues, and can't believe that this break, too, must be made, that this bond, too, must be severed.

Slowly in the course of time, a feeling inside me had come to oppose my unconditional acceptance of my friend Pistorius as a guide. My friendship with him, his advice, his consolation, his proximity were what I had experienced in the most important months of my life as a young man. God had spoken to me through him. From his lips, my dreams had come back to me, explained and interpreted. He had bestowed on me the courage to find myself.—And now, oh! I gradually felt increasing resistance to him. I heard too much in his words of an instructive nature; I felt that he had a firm understanding of one part of me only.

There was no argument or scene between us, no break and not even a squaring of accounts. I merely spoke a single, actually harmless, phrase to him—but nevertheless, at that very moment, an illusion we had shared was shattered into multicolored shards.

For some time the foreboding had oppressed me; it became a distinct feeling one Sunday in his old scholarly room. We were lying on the floor in front of the fire, and he was speaking about mystery cults and religious forms that he was studying and meditating on, and whose possible future occupied his thoughts. But to me all that seemed more of an interesting curiosity than something significant for one's life; I heard in it scholarship, I heard it in a weary search amid the ruins of worlds gone by. And all at once I felt repelled by this whole genre, by this cult of mythologies, by this jigsaw puzzle of handed-own forms of faith.

"Pistorius," I suddenly said, with a malice that surprised even me as it burst forth terrifyingly, "you ought to tell me a dream again sometime, a real dream you had at night. What you're saying now is so—so damned antiquarian!"

He had never heard me talk like that, and at the very moment, I realized in a flash with shame and fright that the arrow I had shot at him, striking him to the heart, had been taken from his own arsenal—that I had now maliciously hurled at him in a more pointed form his own self-reproaches, which I had occasionally heard him utter ironically.

He felt it at once, and fell silent that very moment. I looked at him with fear in my heart and I saw him turn frightfully pale.

After a long, difficult pause he placed fresh wood on the fire and said quietly: "You're quite right, Sinclair, you're a bright fellow. I'll spare you the antiquarian stuff."

He was speaking very calmly, but I could detect the pain of his injury. What had I done?

I was close to tears, I wanted to turn to him cordially, I wanted to ask his forgiveness, to assure him of my love, my tender gratitude. I thought of some touching words—but I couldn't utter them. I remained lying there, looking into the fire in silence. And he was silent, too, and so we lay there, and the fire burned down and collapsed, and as each yelping flame died away I felt something beautiful and intimate dimming and scattering like sparks, with no possibility of return.

"I'm afraid you've misunderstood me," I finally said in a very strained way and in a dry, hoarse voice. The stupid, meaningless words passed my lips as if mechanically, as if I were reading aloud from a serialized novel in the newspaper.

"I understand you perfectly well," said Pistorius quietly. "And you're right." He paused. Then he continued slowly: "As far as any person can be with regard to someone else."

No, no, a voice in me called, I'm wrong!—but I couldn't say a thing. I knew that my single brief phrase had pointed out to him an essential weakness, his distress and wound. I had touched on the spot where he had to distrust himself. His ideal was "antiquarian," he was a seeker into the past, he was a romantic. And suddenly I felt deep down: precisely what Pistorius had been to me and had given me, he couldn't be to himself and give himself. He had led me along a path that had to go beyond even him, the guide, and leave him behind.

Only God knows how a person comes to say such things! I hadn't meant it unkindly, I hadn't had any foreboding of a catastrophe. I had uttered something that at the moment of utterance I wasn't at all aware of; I had yielded to the temptation of a small remark, a little humorous, a little malicious, and it had turned into something fateful. I had committed a small, thoughtless act of rudeness, and for him, it had become a judgment.

Oh, how I wished at the time that he would get angry, defend himself, yell at me! He did none of that; I had to do it all myself, in my own mind. He would have smiled if he had been able to. His inability to do so showed me most clearly how deeply I had hurt him.

And by accepting so silently the blow that I, his impudent and ungrateful pupil, had dealt him; by remaining silent and indicating that I was in the right; by acknowledging my words to be the voice of fate, Pistorius made me hate myself, he made my thoughtlessness a thousand times worse: When I struck, I thought

I was hitting a strong man capable of defending himself—but it was a quiet, suffering man, unarmed, who surrendered in silence.

For quite a while we remained lying in front of the dying fire, in which every glowing figure, every curling rod of ashes, reminded me of happy, beautiful, rich hours, and increased more and more my debt of obligation to Pistorius. Finally, I could no longer stand it. I got up and left. For some time I stood in front of the door in his room; for some time, on the dark stairs; for some time, even in front of the house, waiting for him to come and follow me. Then I proceeded onward, walking for hours and hours through the town and its suburbs, park and forest, until evening. And then, for the first time, I felt the mark of Cain on my forehead.

Only gradually did I begin reflecting on what had happened. All my thoughts had the intention of accusing myself and defending Pistorius. And they all ended with the opposite. A thousand times I was ready to regret my hasty words and take them back—but they had nevertheless been true. It was only then that I succeeded in understanding Pistorius, in constructing his entire dream before my eyes. That dream had been to be a priest, to proclaim the new religion, to offer new forms of edification, love, and worship, to set up new symbols. But that was beyond his powers, it wasn't his office. He dwelt too lovingly in the past, his knowledge of what had once occurred was too precise, he knew too much about Egypt, India, Mithra, Abraxas. His love was attached to images that the world had already seen, and at the same time, he surely knew in his mind that those new things had to be new and different, that they must gush up out of fresh soil and not be drawn from collections and libraries, as if from some old well. His office, perhaps, was to help guide people to themselves, as he had done for me. To give them something altogether novel, their new gods, was not his office.

And at that point the realization suddenly burned me like a searing flame: For each person, there was an "office," but for nobody there was one that he was permitted to choose for himself, to define, and to fill according to his own wishes. It was wrong to desire new gods, it was totally wrong to try and give the world anything! There was no duty for enlightened people, none, none, except this: to seek themselves, to become certain of themselves, to grope forward along their own path, wherever it might lead.—I was deeply affected by that, and for me, that was the profit from that experience. I had often played with images of the future, I had dreamt of roles that might be meant for me, as a poet, perhaps, or as a prophet, or as a painter, or whatever else. That was all meaningless. I didn't exist to write poetry, to preach sermons, to paint pictures; neither I nor anyone else existed for that purpose. All of that merely happened to a person along the way. Everyone had only one true vocation: to find himself. Let him wind up as a poet or a madman, as a prophet or a criminal—that wasn't his business; in the long run, it was irrelevant. His business was to discover his own destiny, not just any destiny, and to live it totally and undividedly. Anything else was just a half-measure, an attempt to run away, an escape back to the ideal of the masses, an adaptation, fear of one's own nature. Fearsome and sacred, the new image rose up before me; I had sensed it a hundred times, perhaps I had already enunciated it, but now I was experiencing it for the first time. I was a gamble of Nature, a throw of the dice into an uncertain realm, leading perhaps to something new, perhaps to nothing; and to let this throw from the primordial depths take effect, to feel it will inside myself and adopt it completely as my own will: that alone was my vocation. That alone!

I had already experienced plenty of loneliness. Now I sensed that even deeper loneliness existed, and that it was inescapable.

I did not attempt to patch things up with Pistorius. We remained friends, but our relationship had changed. Once only we spoke about it; actually, it was only he that did so. He said: "I have the desire to become a priest, as you know. I wanted most of all to become the priest of the new religion that we have so many presentations of. I'll never be able to—I know that, and I've known it for a long time, though I never fully admitted it to myself. Well, I'll perform other priestly duties, perhaps as an organist, perhaps in other ways. But I must always be surrounded by something I feel to be beautiful and holy, organ music and mystery cult, symbol and myth; I need it and I won't give it up.—That's my weakness. Because I know at times, Sinclair, I know sometimes that I shouldn't have such desires, that they represent luxury and weakness. It would be grander, it would be more proper, if I quite simply placed myself at the disposal of fate, making no claims. But I can't; it's the only thing I can't do. Maybe you'll be able to some day. It's difficult, it's the only really difficult thing that exists, my young friend. I've often dreamed of it, but I can't do it, it terrifies me: I can't stand there so completely naked and alone; I, too, am a poor, weak dog that needs a little warmth and food, and would occasionally like to feel the nearness of his own kind. The person who truly wants nothing except his destiny no longer has others of his own kind; he stands completely alone and has only the chill of outer space around him. You know, that's Jesus in the garden of Gethsemane. There have been martyrs who gladly let themselves be crucified, but even they were no heroes and weren't liberated; even they wanted something that they had come to love, that was familiar to them from home; they had models to follow, they had ideals. The person who desires nothing else but destiny no longer has either models or ideals, nothing dear to him, nothing to console him! And that is the right path to follow. People like you and me are really lonely, it's true, but we still have one another, we have the secret satisfaction of being different, of rebelling, of desiring the unusual. That, too, must fall by the wayside if a person wants to follow the path to its end. He mustn't even desire to be a revolutionary, a role model, or a martyr. It's beyond imagining—"

Yes, it was beyond imagining. But it could be dreamed, it could be anticipated, it could be sensed. A few times I had an inkling of it when I found an hour of complete calm. Then I looked into myself and into the wide-open eyes of my fateful image. They could be full of wisdom, they could be full of madness, they could radiate love or deep malice, it made no difference. A person wasn't allowed to choose any of that, he wasn't allowed to want anything. He was only allowed to want himself, his own destiny. Pistorius had served me as a guide for the stretch of the path that led up to that point.

In those days I ran around like a blind man; a storm roared in me, every step I took spelled danger. I saw nothing but the precipitous darkness in front of me, in which all paths I had previously taken petered out and submerged. And in my mind, I saw the image of the guide who resembled Demian, and in whose eyes my destiny lay.

I wrote on a piece of paper: "One guide has left me. I'm completely in the dark. I can't take a step by myself. Help me!"

I wanted to send it to Demian. But I didn't; every time I wanted to, it looked silly and pointless. But I knew that brief prayer by heart and often recited it to myself. It accompanied me at all times. I began to sense the meaning of prayer.

My years of secondary school were over. I was to take a trip during summer vacation, my father had come up with the idea, and then I went to the university. To which faculty, I didn't know. I was granted a semester in the philosophy faculty. I would have been just as content with any other.

CHAPTER 7

LADY EVE

During vacation, I paid a visit to the house in which Max Demian had lived with his mother years before. An old lady was walking in the garden; I spoke to her and learned that the house was hers. I asked about the Demian family. She remembered them well. But she didn't know where they were living at the time. Since she noticed my interest, she invited me into the house, where she found a leather-bound album and showed me a photo of Demian's mother. I could scarcely remember her anymore. But when I looked at the little portrait, my heart stood still. It was my dream image! There it was, the tall, almost masculine female figure, resembling her son, with traces of motherhood, traces of severity, traces of deep passion, beautiful and alluring, beautiful and unapproachable, daemon and mother, destiny and beloved. It was her!

A wild feeling of the miraculous ran through me when I learned that my dream image lived and existed on earth! There really was a woman who looked like that, who bore the features of my destiny! Where was she? Where? And she was Demian's mother.

Shortly thereafter I set out on my trip. A strange trip! I rode unceasingly from place to place, pursuing each and every new idea, constantly searching for that woman. There were days when every figure I saw reminded me of her, hinted at her, resembled her, lured me through streets of unfamiliar cities, through railroad stations, onto trains, as if in complicated dreams. There were other days when I realized how futile my search was; then I would sit idly somewhere in a park, in a hotel garden, in a waiting room, looking inside myself and trying to vivify the image within me. But it had now been scared off and was hard to capture. I was never able to sleep, it was only on train rides through unknown landscapes that I would doze off for fifteen minutes at a time. Once, in Zurich, a woman set her sights on me, a pretty, somewhat shameless female. I barely noticed her and walked by as if she didn't exist. I would sooner have died on the spot than having taken up with another woman for even an hour.

I felt that my destiny was drawing me onward; I felt that fulfillment was near; and I was crazy with impatience at not being able to do anything about it. Once at a railroad station, I think it was in Innsbruck, I saw at the window of a train just pulling out a figure that reminded me of her, and I was miserable for days. And suddenly the figure appeared to me again in a dream at night; I woke up with the embarrassed, empty feeling of the futility of my chase, and I took the next train back home.

A few weeks later I enrolled in the University of H—. Everything disappointed me. The lecture course on the history of philosophy that I attended was just as spiritless and mechanical as the activities of the young students. Everything was so routine, everyone behaved like everyone else, and the flush of merriment on their boyish faces looked so depressingly vacuous and ready-made! But I was free, my whole day was at my disposal; I lived in a quiet, pretty place nestled in the old walls outside of town, and I had a few volumes of Nietzsche on my table. I lived with him, feeling the solitude of his soul and sensing the fate that drove him on implacably; I suffered along with him and was overjoyed to know that there had been a man who had followed his own path so relentlessly.

Late one evening I was sauntering through town, in the blowing autumn wind, and I heard the student glee clubs singing in the taverns. Through the open windows clouds of tobacco smoke drifted out, and, in a dense outpouring, the singing, loud and firm, but uninspired and lifelessly uniform.

I stood at a street corner listening; from two taverns the ritually performed jollity of youth emerged into the night. Everywhere a sense of community, everywhere squatting together, everywhere a shuffling off of destiny and an escape into the warm togetherness of the herd!

Behind me, two men were walking by slowly. I heard a fragment of their conversation.

"Isn't it exactly like the bachelors' lodge in a primitive village?" one of them said. "Everything is the same, even tattoos are still in fashion.[8] You see: this is Young Europe."

The voice sounded oddly admonitory to me—familiar. I followed those two down the dark street. One was Japanese, small and well dressed; when he stood under a streetlamp, I saw his smiling yellow face gleaming.

Then the other one spoke again.

"Well, it's probably no better with you in Japan. People who don't run after the herd are rare everywhere. Even here there are a few."

---

8. "A sarcastic reference to students' ductile scars."

Each word penetrated me with a joyful alarm. I knew the speaker. It was Demian.

Through the windy night, I followed him and the Japanese down the dark streets, listening to their conversations and enjoying the sound of Demian's voice. It had its old timbre, it had its fine old certainty and calm, and it still had power over me. Everything was all right now. I had found him.

At the end of a suburban street, the Japanese said good night and unlocked a house door. Demian started back the way he had come; I had halted and was awaiting him in the middle of the street. My heart pounding, I saw him come toward me, erect and with a springy step, wearing a brown slicker, a thin walking stick hooked over one arm. Without modifying his even pace, he came right up to me, took off his hat, and showed me the same old bright face with the determined mouth and the peculiar brightness on his broad forehead.

"Demian!" I exclaimed.

He held out his hand to me.

"So, there you are, Sinclair! I've been waiting for you."

"Did you know I was here?"

"I didn't exactly know, but I was hoping for it firmly. I didn't see you until this evening; in fact, you were following us the whole time."

"Then, you recognized me right off?"

"Naturally. To be sure, you've changed. But you have the mark, don't you?"

"The mark? What kind of mark?"

"We used to call it the mark of Cain, if you can still recall. It's our mark. You've always had it, that's why I became your friend. But now it's become more distinct."

"I didn't know. Or, actually, I did. Once I painted a picture of you, Demian, and I was amazed to find that it looked like me, too. Was that the mark?"

"It was. I'm so glad you're back! My mother will be happy, too."

I got frightened.

"Your mother? Is she here? But she doesn't know me."

"Oh, she knows about you. She'll recognize you even if I don't tell her who you are. It's been a long time since you sent any news about yourself."

"Oh, I often wanted to write, but I couldn't. For some time I've felt that I'd surely find you again soon. I've been waiting for it every day."

He linked arms with me and we walked on together. Calm radiated from him and permeated me. Soon we were chatting just as in the past. We recalled our school days, our Confirmation lessons, and even that unfortunate meeting during vacation—the only thing we didn't discuss even now was the earliest and strongest bond between us, that business with Franz Kromer.

Unexpectedly we were in the midst of strange, premonitory conversations. Following that talk between Demian and the Japanese, we had spoken about student life, and from there had gone on to other topics that seemed very remote; but as Demian spoke, it all came together in a tight connection.

He spoke about the European spirit and the keynote of the era. Everywhere, he said, togetherness and the herd instinct were prevalent, but freedom and love were nowhere to be found. All that sense of community, from student societies and glee clubs all the way up to national states, was a compulsive form, it was a community based on anxiety, on fear, on confusion, and was inwardly rotten, old, and close to collapse.

"Community," Demian said, "is a fine thing. But the type we see blossoming all over isn't a true community. It will originate anew, out of the knowledge that individuals have of one another, and for a while it will transform the world. The kind of community we have now is merely herd instinct. People run to one another for shelter because they're afraid of one another—capitalists stick together, workers stick together, scholars stick together! And why are they afraid? A person is afraid only when he isn't at one with himself. They're afraid because they have never accepted themselves. A community consisting exclusively of people afraid of the unknown in themselves! They all feel that the rules they live by are no longer valid, that they're following outdated commandments; neither their religions nor their morality, nothing is suited to what we need. For a century and more, Europe has done nothing but study and build factories! They know exactly how many grams of powder it takes to kill someone, but they don't know how to pray to God, they don't even know how to be content for an hour at a time. Just take a look at a students' tavern like these! Or even a pleasure resort that rich people go to! Hopeless! My dear Sinclair, no serenity can come from any of that. These people who rub elbows so anxiously are filled with fear and filled with malice, none of them trusts anyone else. They cling to ideals that no longer count, and they cast stones at everyone who proclaims a new one. I foresee confrontations. They'll come, believe me, they'll come soon! Naturally, they won't 'improve' the world. Whether the workers kill the factory owners or Russia and Germany shoot at each other, that will only mean a change of ownership. But it won't all be for nothing. It will clearly show just how worthless today's ideals are; there will be a clearing out of Stone Age gods. This world, as it now is, wants to die, it wants to perish, and it will!"

"And what will become of us then?" I asked.

"Us? Oh, maybe we'll perish, too. Even people like us can be killed. But that won't eliminate us. The will of the future will gather around whatever we leave behind, or around those of us who survive. The will of mankind will show itself, that will which for some time our Europe has drowned out with its fairground spiel about technology and science. And then it will be seen that the will of mankind is never the same as that of our current communities, the states and the nations, the organizations and the churches. Rather, Nature's intentions for man are inscribed in individuals, in you and me: They were inscribed in Jesus and in Nietzsche. There will be room for these currents, the only important ones—and naturally, they may take on a different aspect daily—when the communities of today collapse."

Late at night we halted in front of a garden by the river.

"This is where we live," said Demian. "Come see us soon! We're eagerly expecting you."

Happily, I made my way home through the night, which had grown chilly. Here and there homebound students were noisily staggering through the town. I had often observed the contrast between their funny style of merriment and my own solitary life, often with the feeling I was missing something, often sarcastically. But never yet had I felt as I did now, calmly and with secret strength, how little that concerned me, how distant and bygone that world was to me. I recalled officials in my hometown, elderly, dignified gentlemen, who clung to the memories of the college years they had boozed away as if they were souvenirs of a blissful paradise, and who celebrated the same sort of cult of the vanished "freedom" of their student days that poets or other romantics devote to their childhood. It's the same all over! All over, people were seeking "freedom" and "happiness" somewhere behind themselves, out of the sheer fear of being reminded of their own responsibilities and being admonished to travel their own path. For a couple of years, they drank and raised hell, and then they knuckled under and became serious citizens in the civil service. Yes, things were rotten, rotten, among us, and this stupidity of student life was less stupid and harmful than a hundred other kinds.

Yet, when I arrived at my distant lodgings and went to bed, all those thoughts had scattered, and my mind was completely and expectantly occupied by the great promise which that day had made me. As soon as I wished, even the very next day, I was to meet Demian's mother. Let the students frequent their taverns and tattoo their faces; let the world be rotten and await its destruction—what was that to me? I was waiting solely for my destiny to come face to face with me in a new guise.

I slept soundly till late morning. The new day dawned for me as a solemn holiday such as I hadn't experienced since the Christmas holidays of my childhood. I was filled with the deepest unrest, but without any fear. I felt that an important day had dawned for me; I saw and sensed that the world around me was transformed, expectant, full of personal significance, and solemn; even the gently falling autumn rain was beautiful, silent, and full of earnestly joyous holiday music. For the first time, the outside world harmonized perfectly with my inner world—such occasions are a holiday for the soul, and life is worth living. No house, no shop window, no face in the street disturbed me; everything was as it had to be, but it wasn't wearing the empty face of the everyday and familiar; rather, it was expectant Nature, it was reverently ready for destiny. That's how I had seen the world'on the mornings of the major holidays, Christmas and Easter, when I was a little boy. I hadn't known this world could still be so beautiful. I had grown accustomed to live inwardly, and I was resigned to the belief that I had simply lost all feeling for the world outside; to the belief that the loss of those glowing colors was inevitably linked to the loss of childhood, and that to some extent the freedom and adulthood of the soul had to be paid for with the renunciation of that lovely shining. Now I saw delightedly that all of that had merely been covered over and thrown in the shade, and that it was possible, even for a liberated person giving up childish joys, to see the world in its radiance and to taste the intimate thrills of a child's viewpoint.

The hour came when I rediscovered that suburban garden beside which I had taken leave of Max Demian the night before. Concealed behind tall trees that were gray in the rain, stood a small house, bright and cozy, tall flowering plants behind a big glass wall, darkroom walls with pictures and bookshelves behind gleaming windows. The entrance door led directly into a little, heated vestibule; a silent, elderly maid, dark-complexioned, with a white apron, invited me in and took my coat.

She left me alone in the vestibule. I looked around, and at once I was in the midst of my dream. Up on the dark wooden wall, over a door, hung a well-known picture under glass in a dark frame: my bird with the golden-yellow sparrowhawk's head, breaking its way out of the globe. I stood still, deeply moved—my heart was so happy and melancholy at the same time, as if at that moment everything I ever did or lived through was coming back to me in the form of a response and a fulfillment. Quick as a flash I saw a throng of images racing past my soul: my father's house in my hometown with the old stone coat-of-arms at the top of its entrance archway; Demian as a boy drawing the coat-of-arms; myself as a boy fearfully ensnared in my friend Kromer's evil spell; myself as an adolescent painting the bird of my desire at the quiet table in my little student's room, my soul entangled in the web formed by its own threads—and everything, everything down to that very moment, reechoed in my mind, while I affirmed it, responded to it, approved it.

With eyes that had become moist I gazed at my picture and read within myself. Then I looked down: below the picture of the bird, in the now open doorway, stood a tall woman in a dark dress. It was her.

I was unable to say a word. Her face was timeless and ageless like her son's, and similarly filled with enthusiastic willpower, the beautiful, venerable lady was smiling at me amiably. Her gaze spelled fulfillment, her welcome signified homecoming. In silence, I held out my hands to her. She grasped both of them with her own firm, warm hands.

"You're Sinclair. I recognized you at once. Welcome!"

Her voice was deep and warm, so I drank it like sweet wine. And now I looked up at her tranquil face, at her dark, unfathomable eyes, at her vivacious, mature lips, at her open, princely forehead, which bore the mark.

"How happy I am!" I told her, kissing her hands. "I think that all my life I've always been on a journey—and now I've arrived home."

She gave me a maternal smile.

"No one ever arrives home," she said amiably. "But when the paths of friends meet, the whole world looks like home for a while."

She expressed what I had felt on my way to meet her. Her voice and even her words were very similar to her son's, and yet quite different. It was all more mature, warmer, more self-evident. But, just as Max years ago had never given anyone the impression that he was a young boy, in the same way, his mother didn't look like the mother of a grown son, the aura of her face and hair was so young and sweet, her golden skin so taut and unwrinkled, her mouth so rosy. She stood before me looking even more regal than in my dream, and her proximity was love's happiness, her gaze was fulfillment.

And so this was the new guise in which my destiny revealed itself to me, no longer severe, no longer making me lonely—no, ripe and pleasure-laden! I made no decisions, I took no vow—I had arrived at a goal, at an elevated stopping place on my journey, from which the continuation of the path was revealed in its length and splendor, striving toward promised lands, shaded by treetops of nearby happiness, cooled by the nearby gardens of all sorts of pleasure. Let things go with me as they might, I was blissful just knowing that this woman existed, just drinking in her voice and inhaling her presence. Let her become my mother, my beloved, my goddess—as long as she was there, as long as my path was close to hers!

She pointed up at my picture of the sparrowhawk.

"You never gave our Max greater pleasure than with this picture," she said reflectively. "And to me, too. We've waited for you, and when the picture came we knew you were on the way to us. When you were a little boy, Sinclair, one day my son came home from school and said: 'There's a boy who has the mark on his forehead; he's got to become my friend.' That was you. You didn't have an easy time of it, but we trusted you. Once, when you were home on vacation, you met Max again. At the time you were about sixteen. Max told me about it—"

I interrupted her: "Oh, I'm sorry he told you that! I was then going through my most miserable phase!"

"Yes, Max said to me: 'Now Sinclair has his hardest time ahead of him. He's trying once more to escape into society, he's even become a tavern goer; but he won't succeed. His mark is hidden, but it burns him in secret.' Wasn't that so?"

"Oh, yes, it was so, precisely so. Then I found Beatrice, and then finally another guide came my way. His name was Pistorius. Only then did it become clear to me why my boyhood was so closely linked to Max, why I couldn't break away from him. Dear lady—dear Mother, I often thought at the time that I'd have to kill myself. Is everyone's path that difficult?"

She stroked my hair with a hand that was light as air.

"It's always difficult to be born. As you know, the bird must make an effort to break out of the egg. Think back and ask: Was the path really that difficult? Merely difficult? Wasn't it also beautiful? Could you have thought of a more beautiful or easier one?"

I shook my head.

"It was difficult," I said, as if asleep, "it was difficult until the dream came."

She nodded and looked at me penetratingly.

"Yes, one must find one's dream, then the path becomes easy. But no dream lasts forever, each one is replaced by a new one, and you shouldn't try to hold onto any of them."

I was severely frightened. Was that already a warning? Was that already a rejection? But I didn't care; I was ready to let myself be guided by her, without asking what the goal was.

"I don't know how long my dream will last," I said. "I wish it were eternal. Below is the picture of the bird my destiny has welcomed me, like a mother, and like a beloved. I belong to my destiny and to no one else."

"As long as the dream is your destiny, you must remain faithful to it," she said, in earnest confirmation of my words.

A sadness seized on me, and the ardent desire to die at that enchanted hour. I felt tears—how infinitely long it had been since I last wept! Jing up in my eyes uncontrollably and overpowering me. I turned away from her violently, walked over to the window, and looked out over the flowerpots with unseeing eyes.

Behind me I heard her voice; it sounded calm and yet it was as full of tenderness as a goblet filled to the brim with wine.

"Sinclair, you're a child! You know that your destiny loves you. One day it will be all yours, just as in your dreams, if you remain faithful."

I had regained control of myself, and I turned my face to her again. She gave me her hand.

"I have a few friends," she said with a smile, "a few very rare, very close friends who call me Lady Eve. You may call me that, too, if you like."

She led me to the door, opened it, and indicated the garden. "You'll find Max out there."

Beneath the tall trees, I stood numb and shaken, more awake or deeper in dreams than ever, I didn't know which. Quietly the rain was dripping from the boughs. I walked slowly into the garden, which extended far along the riverbank. Finally, I found Demian. He was standing in a little open garden building, stripped to the waist, practicing boxing with a sand-filled bag that was suspended there.

I halted in amazement. Demian looked marvelous, with a broad chest and a firm, manly head; his raised arms, with their taut muscles, were strong and capable; his movements sprang like playing fountains from his hips, upper back, and shoulder joints.

"Demian!" I called. "What are you doing there?"

He laughed merrily.

"I'm practicing. I promised the little Japanese a wrestling match; the guy is as nimble as a cat and naturally just as sly.

But he won't beat me. It's kind of humbling that I owe him in a very small way."

He pulled on his shirt and jacket.

"You've already met my mother?" he asked.

"Yes. Demian, what a splendid mother you have! Lady Eve! The name suits her perfectly, she's like the mother of all beings."

He looked into my face reflectively for a moment.

"You already know that name? You have a right to be proud, young man! You're the first person she's ever told it to right from the outset."

From that day on, I frequented that house like a son and brother, but also like a lover. When I closed the gate behind me, yes, as soon as I saw the tall trees in the garden looming up in the distance, I felt rich and happy. Outside, "reality" existed; outside there were streets and houses, people and their institutions, libraries and lecture halls—but here there was love, soul; here, fairy tale and dream dwelt. And yet our life was by no means cut off from the world, in our thoughts and conversations we often lived right in the midst of it, but on another plane; we were separated from the majority of people not by frontiers but merely by a different way of seeing. Our task was to represent an island in the world, perhaps a model to be followed, but at any rate to make our life the annunciation of a different possibility. I, who had been solitary for so long, became acquainted with the society that is possible among people who have experienced total isolation. Never again did I desire to return to the banquets of the fortunate, the feasts of the happy; never again was I assailed by envy or homesickness when I observed the societies of others. And slowly I was initiated into the mystery of those who bore "the mark" on their person.

We who bore the mark might well be considered by the rest of the world as strange, even as insane and dangerous. We had awoken, or were awaking, and we were striving for an ever more perfect state of wakefulness, whereas the ambition and quest for happiness of the others consisted of linking their opinions, ideals, and duties, their life and happiness, ever more closely with those of the herd. They, too, strove; they, too, showed signs of strength and greatness. But, as we saw it, whereas we marked men represented Nature's determination to create something new, individual, and forward-looking, the others lived in the determination to stay the same. For them mankind—which they loved as much as we did—was a fully formed entity that had to be preserved and protected. For us mankind was a distant future toward which we were all journeying, whose aspect no one knew, whose laws weren't written down anywhere.

Besides Lady Eve, Max, and me, our circle included many other questers of very different kinds, some closer to us, some more distant. Many of them traveled special paths, had set unusual goals for themselves, and were adherents of special opinions and duties; among them were astrologers and kabbalists, even a follower of Count Tolstoy, and all sorts of gentle, shy, vulnerable people, followers of new sects, practitioners of Hindu yoga, vegetarians, and others. Actually, we had nothing in common intellectually with all these people except the respect each of them accorded to the secret life's dream of the others. Others were closer to us, those who pursued mankind's quest for gods and new ideals in the past, and whose studies often reminded me of those of Pistorius. They brought along books, translated texts in ancient languages for us, showed us illustrations of old symbols and rites, and taught us to see that mankind's entire treasury of ideals up to now has consisted of the dreams of the unconscious soul, dreams in which mankind has grudgingly followed the premonitions of its culture possibilities. And so we ranged through the ancient world's marvelous, thousand-headed cluster of gods all the way to the dawning of the great change represented by Christianity. We became familiar with the creeds of pious anchors and the changes in religions from one nation to another. And from all we collected we derived a critique of our own age and present-day Europe, which through mighty efforts had created powerful new weapons for mankind, but had finally fallen into a deep and at last blatant spiritual desolation. For it had gained the whole world, while losing its soul in the process.

Here, too, there were believers and confessors of well-defined hopes and doctrines of salvation. There were Buddhists who wanted to convert Europe, and disciples of Tolstoy, and other creeds. We in the narrower circle listened but accepted none of these doctrines as anything but symbols. We marked men who were not at all worried about the shape the future would take. To us every credo, every doctrine of salvation seemed stillborn and useless. And there was only one thing we conceived as our duty and destiny: for each of us to become so completely himself, so completely in harmony with the creative germ of Nature within himself, living in accordance with its commands, that the uncertain future would find us ready for any eventuality, whatever it might bring.

For this, whether spoken or unspoken, was clear in all our minds: that a rebirth, and the collapse of what now existed, was near and already perceptible. Demian said to me at times: "What will come is beyond imagining. The soul of Europe is an animal that has lain in fetters for an infinitely long time. When it is freed, its first impulses won't be of the most charming kind. But its paths and byways don't matter as long as the true distress of its soul is revealed, that distress which for so long has again and again been falsely denied and anesthetized. That will be our day, then we'll be needed, not as guides or new legislators—we won't live to see the new laws—but as willing people, people are ready to go along and take a stand where destiny calls them. Look, all people are ready to accomplish unbelievable things when their ideals are threatened. But no one's there when a new ideal, a new, possibly dangerous and unfamiliar stirring of growth knocks at the door. We will be those few who are there and go along. That's what we're marked for—as Cain was marked to arouse fear and hatred, and to drive the people of those days out of their idyllic narrow confines into perilous distances. All the people who have affected the course of mankind, all of them without exception, were only capable and influential because they were prepared for their destiny. That goes for Moses and Buddha, it goes for Napoleon and Bismarck. Whichever movement a person serves, whichever pole governs his actions, is not for him to choose. If Bismarck had understood the Social Democrats and had adapted his policies to them, he would have been a smart man, but not a man of destiny. And so it was with Napoleon, with Caesar, with Loyola, with all of them! That must always be conceived of in the biological and evolutionary sense! When the enormous changes on the earth's surface drove aquatic animals onto land and terrestrial animals into the water, it was the individuals ready for their destiny that were able to accomplish new, unheard of things and to save their species by means of new adaptations. Whether the rescuers were the individuals that had earlier been outstanding in their species as conservatives and preservers of old ways, or whether the eccentrics and revolutionaries saved the species, we don't know. They were ready, and thus able to preserve the life of the species for the necessary new developments. That we do know. Therefore we want to be ready."

Lady Eve was often present during such discussions, but she did not speak in that fashion. For each of us who uttered his thoughts, she was a listener and echo, full of trust, full of comprehension; it was as if all our thoughts originated in her and returned to her. To sit near her, to hear her voice occasionally, and to share in the atmosphere of soulful maturity that surrounded her was happiness to me.

She immediately sensed any change, dullness of spirit, or renewal that might be taking place in me. I felt as if my dreams at night were inspiration coming from her. I often recounted them to her, and she found them comprehensible and natural; there was no peculiar feature that she couldn't follow with clear discernment. For a time I had dreams that were like reconstructions of the conversations we had had during the day. I dreamt that the whole world was in an uproar and that I, either alone or with Demian, was waiting in suspense for that great destiny. The destiny remained hidden, but somehow it bore the features of Lady Eve—to be chosen or rejected by her: that was destiny.

Sometimes she said with a smile: "Your dream isn't complete, Sinclair, you've forgotten the best part" and then at times I remembered the rest and couldn't understand how I could have forgotten it.

Occasionally I became dissatisfied and tortured by desires. I thought I could no longer abide by her next to me without taking her in my arms. That, too, she would notice at once. When I once stayed away for several days and then returned all upset, she took me aside and said: "You shouldn't surrender yourself to wishes you don't believe in. I know what you desire. You must be able to give up those wishes, or else desire them completely and firmly. If some day you are able to make the request feeling quite certain it will be granted, then it will actually be granted. But you make wishes and then regret them, feeling afraid all the while. But you have to get over that. I'll tell you a tale."

And she told me about a young man who was in love with a star. He stood by the sea, held out his hands, and worshipped the star; he dreamt about it and turned his thoughts to it. But he knew, or thought he knew, that a star couldn't be embraced by a human being. He deemed it his fate to love a heavenly body with no hope of being requited, and on the basis of that notion he constructed an entire poetics of life consisting of renunciation and silent, faithful suffering, which was to improve him and purify him. But all his dreams were of the star. Once he was standing by the sea again at night, on the high cliff, looking up at the star and blazing with love for it. And in a moment of supreme longing he jumped and plunged into the void, in the direction of the star. But at the moment he jumped he still thought, quick as a flash: "But it's impossible!" There he lay, down on the beach, shattered. He didn't know how to love. If, at the moment he jumped, he had had the psychic strength to believe firmly and certainly that his love would be requited, he would have flown into the sky to be united with the star.

"Love ought not to make requests," she said, "but shouldn't make demands, either. Love must have the strength to reach certainty for itself. Then it no longer undergoes the power of attraction, but exerts it. Sinclair, your love is being attracted to me. Whenever it begins to attract me, I shall come. I don't want to make a gift for myself, I want to win."

But another time she told me another tale. It was about a man who loved without hope. He withdrew completely inside himself, and thought he would burn up with love. He lost contact with the world; he no longer saw the blue sky and the green forest; the brook didn't murmur for him, the harp didn't sound for him; everything had gone under, and he had become poor and miserable. But his love grew, and he was much more ready to die and wither away than to renounce the possession of the beautiful woman he loved. Then he noticed that his love had burnt up everything else in him; it became powerful and exerted more and more attraction; and the beautiful woman was compelled to follow; she came, he stood there with outstretched arms to draw her to himself. But when she stood before him, she was totally transformed, and with trembling he felt and saw that he had attracted to himself the entire world he had lost. It stood before him and yielded itself to him; sky and forest and brook, everything came to meet him in new colors, vivid and splendid; it belonged to him, it spoke his language. And instead of merely winning a woman, he had the whole world in his bosom, and every star in the sky shone within him and sparkled joy into his soul.—He had loved and, by doing so, had found himself. But most people love to lose themselves.

My love for Lady Eve seemed like the only thing my life contained. But every day it took on a different aspect. Sometimes I was sure I felt that it wasn't her physical person that my whole being was drawn to and strove to win, but that she was only a symbol of my inner self, and she was trying merely to lead me deeper into myself. Often I heard her say things that sounded like answers given by my unconscious burning questions that were agitating me. Then again, there were moments when I was aflame with sensuous desire in her presence, and I kissed objects she had touched. And gradually the sensuous and the nonsensuous love, the reality and the symbol, began to overlap. At such times I would think of her back in my room, in the calm lovingness, while I thought I could feel her hand in mine and her lips on mine. Or else I was with her, looking at her face, talking with her and hearing her voice, and yet unsure whether she was real and not a dream. I began to sense how someone can possess a permanent, immortal love. While reading a book I gained a new insight, and it was the same feeling as being kissed by Lady Eve. She stroked my hair, and her mature, fragrant warmth emanated from her smile, and I had the same feeling as if I had made some spiritual progress. Everything important and fateful for me was capable of assuming her form. She could transform herself into each of my thoughts, and each of them could be transformed into her.

I had been dreading Christmas vacation, when I would be with my parents, because I thought it would surely be torture to be away from Lady Eve for two weeks. But it was no torture, it was wonderful to be home and to think about her. When I was back in H—, I stayed away from her house for two more days in order to enjoy this sense of security and freedom from dependence on her physical presence. I also had dreams in which my union with her took place in new, metaphorical ways. She was an ocean, and a river flowing into it. She was a star, and another star journeying toward her; we met and felt each other's attraction, stayed together, and revolved around each other blissfully for all eternity in close, musical orbits.

I told her that dream the first time I visited her again. "It's a beautiful dream," she said quietly. "Make it come true!"

There came a day in early spring that I've never forgotten. I stepped into the vestibule; a window was open, and a gentle breeze wafted the heavy scent of the hyacinths through the room. Since there was no one to be seen, I went upstairs to Max Demian's study. I knocked softly at the door and went in without waiting for a response, just as I had become accustomed to do.

The room was dark, all the curtains were drawn. The door to a little side room, where Max had installed a chemistry lab, was open. From there came the bright white light of the springtime sun that's shining through rain clouds. I thought no one was there, and I drew back one of the drapes.

Then I saw Max Demian sitting on a stool close to the curtained window; he was hunched up and strangely altered, and in a flash, the thought ran through me: "You've experienced this before!" His arms were hanging motionless, his hands were in his lap, his face was leaning a little forward, his open eyes were unseeing and lifeless, and his rigid pupils reflected a small spot of harsh light, as a piece of glass would. His pallid face was sunken in and had no expression except that of horrible immobility; it looked like an age-old animal mask on the portal of a temple. He didn't seem to be breathing.

I felt a thrill of recollection—I had once seen him looking exactly like that, years before when I was still a young boy. That's how his eyes had stared inwardly, that's how his hands had lain together lifelessly, a fly had crawled over his face. And at the time, some six years before, he had looked just as old and timeless, not a wrinkle in his face was different today.

Assailed by fear, I stepped softly out of the room and walked downstairs. In the vestibule, I met Lady Eve. She was pale and seemed weary, in a way I didn't associate with her; a shadow passed through the window; the harsh white sunlight had suddenly disappeared.

"I was with Max," I whispered rapidly. "Has anything happened? He's asleep, or meditating, I don't know which; I saw him this way once before."

"I hope you didn't awaken him," she said quickly.

"No. He didn't hear me. I went right out again. Lady Eve, tell me, "What's wrong with him?"

She drew the back of her hand across her forehead.

"Be calm, Sinclair, nothing's happening to him. He has withdrawn. It won't last long."

She stood up and went out into the garden, even though it was just starting to rain. I was aware that she didn't want me to accompany her. And so I paced to and fro in the vestibule, smelling the numbingly fragrant hyacinths, gazing at my painted bird over the door, and breathing in anxiously the strange shade that filled the house that morning. What was it? What had happened?

Lady Eve soon returned. Raindrops hung in her dark hair. She sat down in her armchair. Weariness was upon her. I stepped up to her, leaned over her, and kissed away the drops from her hair. Her eyes were bright and calm, but the drops tasted like tears.

"Should I see how he is?" I asked in a whisper.

She smiled faintly.

"Don't be a child, Sinclair!" she admonished me loudly, as if she wanted to break a spell she was under. "Leave now and come back later, I can't talk with you now."

I left and escaped from my house and town in the direction of the hills; the thin rain fell on me obliquely; the clouds scudded as if in fear, low in the sky, under heavy pressure. Down below there was hardly any wind, but up in the hills a storm seemed to be raging; several times the pale, harsh sunlight momentarily broke through the steely gray of the clouds.

Then a fluffy yellow cloud came drifting across the sky; it condensed against that gray wall, and in a few seconds the wind formed an image out of the yellow and blue, a gigantic bird that tore itself out of the blue chaos and with broad wing beats disappeared into the sky. Then the storm became audible, and rain mixed with hail rattled down. A brief clap of thunder, with a frightening and improbably loud noise, crashed over the rain-lashed countryside, immediately thereafter a glimpse of sun broke through, and on the nearby mountains pale snow gleamed in unreal pallor above the brown woods.

When I returned hours later, wet and wind-blown, Demian himself opened the door to the house.

He brought me up to his room; in the lab a gas flame was burning, papers were scattered around, he seemed to have been working.

"Sit down," he said invitingly, "you must be tired; it was a terrible storm, and I can see you were out in the midst of it. Tea is on the way."

"Something is happening today," I began hesitantly. "It can't be only this little storm."

He looked at me inquiringly.

"Have you seen anything?"

"Yes. For a moment I saw an image distinctly in the clouds."

"What sort of image?"

"It was a bird."

"The sparrowhawk? Was it that? Your dream bird?"

"Yes, it was my sparrowhawk. It was yellow and gigantic, and it flew into the dark blue sky."

Demian heaved a deep sigh.

There was a knock. The elderly maid was bringing tea,

"Take some, Sinclair, please. I believe you didn't see the bird merely by chance?"

"By chance? Do people see things like that by chance?"

"You're right, they don't. It means something. Do you know what?"

"No. I only feel that it means some catastrophe, a step forward in our destiny. I believe it concerns us all."

He was pacing back and forth excitedly.

"A step forward in our destiny!" he shouted. "I had the same kind of dream last night, and yesterday my mother had a premonition that meant the same thing.—I dreamt I was climbing a ladder that was leaning up against a tree trunk or a tower. When I reached the top I saw the whole countryside (it was a wide plain) on fire, with all its towns and villages. I can't tell you all of it yet, not everything is clear to me yet."

"Do you interpret the dream as applying to you?" I asked.

"To me? Of course. Nobody dreams of things that don't concern him. But it doesn't concern me alone, you're right about that. I can make a fairly accurate distinction between dreams that indicate stirrings in my own soul and those very rare ones that point to the destiny of mankind as a whole. I've seldom had such dreams, and never one of which I could say was a prophecy and came true. Interpretations are too uncertain. But this I know for a fact: I've had a dream that doesn't concern me alone. You see, this dream is connected with others that I've had in the past, and it's a continuation of them. It's from these dreams, Sinclair, that I derive the premonitions I've already spoken to you about. We know that the world we live in is thoroughly decayed, but that's not a sufficient reason to prophesy its destruction or something like that. But for several years I've had dreams from which I conclude, or feel, or what have you—let's say, I feel—that the collapse of an old world is moving closer. At first, the premonitions were very weak and remote, but they've become more and more distinct and strong. So far all I know is that something big and terrible is impending, something that concerns me and everybody. Sinclair, we're going to live through the things we've often discussed! The world wants to renew itself. There's a smell of death in the air. No new thing can arrive unless an old thing dies—It's more terrible than I had imagined." I gazed at him in fear.

"Can't you tell me the rest of your dream?" I requested it timidly.

He shook his head.

"No."

The door opened and Lady Eve came in.

"There you are sitting together! Children, you aren't sad, are you?"

She looked lively and no longer tired. Demian smiled at her, and she came over to us, as a mother came to frightened children.

"We're not sad, Mother, we're just puzzled over these new signs a little. But it doesn't matter. Whatever is coming will suddenly be here, and then we'll learn soon enough what we need to know."

But I was in a bad mood, and when I took my leave and was walking through the vestibule alone, I felt that the fragrance of the hyacinths was weak, stale, and corpse-like. A shadow had fallen over us.

CHAPTER 8

The Beginning of the End

I had wangled permission to stay in H—for the summer term, too. Instead of staying in the house, we were now almost always in the garden by the river. The Japanese, who incidentally had lost the wrestling match badly, were gone, as was the Tolstoy disciple. Demian kept a horse and rode untiringly every day. I was often alone with his mother.

At times I was surprised at the peacefulness of my life. I had been so long accustomed to being alone, to practicing resignation, to tussling strenuously with my torments, that those months in H—seemed to me like a dream island on which I could live in comfortable enchantment, devoting myself exclusively to beautiful, pleasant things and ideas. I sensed that it was a foretaste of that new, higher society we were discussing. And occasionally I became very sad over that happiness, because I was well aware it couldn't last. I wasn't meant to exist in the lap of plenty and ease; I needed torment and persecution. I felt that someday I would awaken from those beautiful images of love and once more be alone, all alone, in the cold world of the others, where there was only solitude or struggle for me, not peace or participation.

Then I nestled into Lady Eve's nearness with redoubled tenderness, glad that my destiny still bore those beautiful, calm features.

The summer weeks went by quickly and easily, the term was already finished. It was almost time to say goodbye; it would have been wrong for me to think about it, and I didn't; rather, I clung to those lovely days as a butterfly clings to the honey flower. That had been my time of happiness, the first fulfilling time in my life, and my acceptance into the group—what would come next? I would once again fight my way through, suffer from longing, dream dreams, be alone.

On one of those days, I was so greatly overcome by that premonitory feeling that my love for Lady Eve suddenly flared up painfully. My God, just a little while and I wouldn't be seeing her, wouldn't be hearing her firm, lovable steps in the house, wouldn't be finding her flowers on my table! And what had I accomplished? I had dreamed and cradled myself in comfort, instead of winning her, instead of fighting for her and seizing her to be mine forever! Everything she had ever told me about true love now came back to me, a hundred subtle words of exhortation, a hundred gentle allurements, perhaps promises—what had I done with it all? Nothing! Nothing!

I took a stand in the middle of my room, summoned up every ounce of consciousness, and thought about Eve. I wanted to gather all the strength of my soul, so that she would feel my love, so that she would be compelled to come to me. She had to come and long for my embrace until she won it, my kisses must burrow insatiably into her ripe, loving lips.

I stood there harnessing my powers until a chill spread through me, starting with my fingers and feet. I felt strength emanating from me. For a few moments something inside me contracted firmly and tightly, something bright and cool; for a moment I had the sensation of carrying a crystal in my heart, and I knew it was myself. The cold reached my breast.

When I awoke from that frightening exertion, I sensed that something was on its way to me. I was dead with exhaustion, but I was prepared to see Eve walk into the room, ardent and rapturous.

Now a clatter of hooves hammered up the long street; it sounded close and metallic; all at once, it stopped. I leaped to the window. Below, Demian was dismounting. I ran downstairs.

"What's going on, Demian? I hope nothing has happened to your mother!"

He didn't listen to what I was saying. He was very pale, and from both sides of his forehead sweat was running down his cheeks. He tied the reins of his horse, which was hot from running, to the garden fence; he took my arm and walked down the street with me.

"Have you already heard something?"

I didn't know a thing.

Demian squeezed my arm and turned his face to me, with a dark, sympathetic, odd look.

"Yes, my friend, it has started. I'm sure you knew about our very strained relations with Russia."

"What? Are we at war? I never thought it would happen."

He spoke quietly, even though there was no one else around.

"It hasn't been declared yet. But the war is on. Rely on it. Since that other time, I haven't bothered you about this business, but in the meantime, I've seen new omens three times. And so, it won't be the end of the world, or an earthquake, or a revolution. It will be a war. You'll see how popular It will be! People will be in raptures, even now everybody's looking forward to a scrap. That's how dull their life has become. But you'll see, Sinclair, this is just the beginning. Maybe it'll turn into a big war, a very big war. But even that is only the beginning. New times are dawning, and for those who cling to the old, the new will be horrible. What are you going to do?"

I was bewildered; it all still sounded strange and improbable to me.

"I don't know—and you?"

He shrugged his shoulders.

"As soon as they announce mobilization, I'll be in the army. I'm a lieutenant."

"You? I didn't know a thing about it."

"Yes, it was one of my ways of adapting. As you know, I've never wanted to be conspicuous outwardly, and I've always preferred to do a little too much in order to be correct. I think that in a week I'll already be at the front."

"For the love of God."

"Now, now, my boy, you mustn't get sentimental about it. Basically, of course, I won't get much pleasure out of ordering my men to fire at living people, but that will be secondary. Now each of us will get caught up in the big wheel. You, too. You'll definitely be drafted."

"And your mother, Demian?"

Only at that point did I recall what had been going on fifteen minutes earlier. How the world has changed! I had been concentrating all my strength in order to conjure up the sweetest image, and now destiny was suddenly staring at me in a new form from a menacingly horrid mask.

"My mother? Oh, we don't need to worry about her. She's safe, safer than anyone else in the world today. -- You love her that much, then?"

"You knew, Demian?" He laughed cheerfully and unconstrained.

"My little friend! Of course, I knew. No one yet has called my mother Lady Eve unless he was in love with her. By the way, what was going on? Didn't you summon her or me today?"

"Yes, I called—I called Lady Eve."

"She sensed it. She sent me off to see you at once. I had just told her the news about Russia."

We turned back, not saying much more; he untied his horse and mounted it.

It was only when I was upstairs in my room that I noticed how exhausted I was, from Demian's message and even more from my previous exertion. But Lady Eve had heard me! With my thoughts, I had reached her heart. She would have arrived herself—except that—How odd all this was, and, basically, how beautiful! Now a war was upon us. Now all that we had talked about so often was to start happening. And Demian had known so much about it in advance. How strange it was that now the current of the world was no longer going to flow somewhere past us—that it was now suddenly moving right through our hearts, that adventures and wild destinies were summoning us, and that now or soon the moment would come when the world needed us, when it would be transformed. Demian was right, one shouldn't get sentimental about it. The only peculiar thing was that now I would be experiencing "destiny," usually such a personal matter, in common with so many others, with the whole world. Good!

I was prepared. When I walked through town that evening, there was a hubbub of great excitement in every nook and cranny. Everywhere there is the word "war"!

I arrived at Lady Eve's house; we had supper in the little garden house. I was the only guest. No one said a word about the war. Only very late, shortly before I left, did Lady Eve say: "My dear Sinclair, you summoned me today. You know why I didn't come myself. But don't forget: now you know how to call me, and whenever you need someone who bears the mark, call again!"

She stood up and walked ahead of us through the twilight of the garden. The mysterious woman strode, tall and regal, among the silent trees, and above her head shone the numerous stars, small and delicate.

I'm reaching the end. Things took their swift course. Soon the war was declared, and Demian, strangely unfamiliar-looking in the uniform with the silver-gray coat, departed. I escorted his mother back to her home. Soon I, too, said goodbye to her; she kissed my lips and clasped me to her breast for a moment, while her large eyes blazed into mine, close and intensely.

And all people were like brothers. They had the Fatherland and honor in mind. But it was destiny into whose unveiled face they were all gazing for a moment. Young men left their barracks and boarded trains, and on many faces, I saw a mark—not ours—a beautiful, dignified mark signifying love and death. I, too, was hugged by people I had never seen, and I understood and gladly reciprocated. It was an intoxication in which they acted that way, they weren't in harmony with their fate; but the intoxication was holy, it was caused by their all having taken that brief, rousing look into the eyes of destiny.

It was nearly winter by the time I was sent to the front.

In the beginning, despite the sensations aroused by the constant gunfire, I was disappointed in everything. Earlier I had thought a lot about why it was so extremely unusual for a person to be able to live for an ideal. Now I saw that many people, all in fact, are capable of dying for an ideal. Only, it mustn't be a personal, freely chosen ideal, but one held in common and taken over from other people.

But as time went by, I saw that I had underestimated people. Even though military service and their shared danger made them so much alike, nevertheless I saw many, the living and the dying, approach the acceptance of destiny in a splendid manner. Not only while attacking, but all the time, many of them, very many, had that steady, distant, almost obsessed gaze that is not directed at goals but indicates complete surrender to the prodigious. No matter what they chose to believe and think—they were ready, they were useful, the future could be formed from them. And no matter how inflexibly the world was clamoring for war and heroism, honor and other outmoded ideals, no matter how remote and unlikely every voice that apparently spoke up for humanity sounded, all of that was merely superficial, just as the question of the external and political aims of the war remained superficial. Deep down, something was evolving. Something like a new humanity. Because I could see many people, and a number of them died alongside me, who had gained the emotional insight that hatred and rage, killing and destroying, were not linked to the specific objects of that rage. No, the objects, just like the aims, were completely accidental. Those primal feelings, even the wildest of them, weren't directed against the enemy; their bloody results were merely an outward materialization of people's inner life, the split within their souls, which desired to rage and kill, destroy and die, so that they could be reborn. A gigantic bird was fighting its way out of the egg, and the egg was the world, and the world had to fall to pieces.

One early spring night, I was standing guard in front of the farmhouse we had occupied. A listless wind was blowing in capricious gusts; armies of clouds were riding across the high heavens of Flanders; somewhere behind them was a hint of the moon. That whole day I had already been restless; some worry was nagging at me. Now, in my post in the darkness, I was thinking lovingly of the images of my earlier life, of Lady Eve, of Demian. I was leaning against a poplar and gazing at the agitated sky, in which the bright areas, mysteriously shifting, were soon transformed into large, radiating series of images. By the unusual slowness of my pulse, by the insensitivity of my skin to wind and rain, by the sparks of my inner alertness, I felt that a guide was near me.

In the clouds, I could see a great city from which millions of people poured out in swarms over wide stretches of countryside. Into their midst there stepped a powerful divine figure, sparkling stars in its hair, tall as a mountain chain, with the features of Lady Eve. Into that figure, as if into a gigantic cave, the columns of people vanished, and were lost from view. The goddess crouched down on the ground, the mark on her forehead gleaming brightly. A dream seemed to overpower her, she shut her eyes, and her huge face was distorted with pain. Suddenly she screamed shrilly, and from her forehead shot stars, many thousands of radiant stars, which flung themselves across the black sky in splendid arcs and semicircles.

One of the stars whizzed directly toward me with a bright sound; it seemed to be seeking me out. Then, with a roar, it exploded into a thousand sparks; it yanked me upward and threw me to the ground again; with a thunderclap, the world collapsed above me.

I was found near the poplar covered with earth and wounded in many places.

I was lying in a cellar, cannons were roaring overhead. I was lying on a cart, bumping over empty fields. Most of the time I slept or was unconscious. But the more soundly I slept, the more violently I felt that something was drawing me onward, that I was following a power that had gained mastery over me.

I was lying in a stable on straw; it was dark; someone had stepped on my hand. But my inner self wanted to move on, I felt a stronger pull away from there. Again I was lying in a cart and, later, on a stretcher or ladder; I had a stronger and stronger feeling that I was being intentionally conveyed somewhere; all I felt was the urge to get there finally.

Then I reached my destination. It was nighttime, I was fully conscious; I had just still felt that pull and urge in me powerfully. Now I was lying in a large room, bedded down on the floor and I had the feeling that I was where I had been summoned to. I looked around; right next to my mattress was another one, with someone on it who was leaning forward and looking at me. He had the mark on his forehead. It was Max Demian.

I was unable to speak, and he, too, was unable or unwilling to. He just looked at me. On his face was the glow from a light-bulb that hung above him on the wall. He smiled at me.

For an infinitely long time, he kept looking into my eyes. Slowly he moved his face closer to me until we were almost touching.

"Sinclair," he said in a whisper.

I signaled him with my eyes that understood him.

He smiled again, almost as if in sympathy.

"My young friend!" he said with a smile.

Now his mouth was right next to mine. He continued speaking quietly.

"Can you still recall Franz Kromer?" he asked.

I winked at him, and I managed to smile, too.

"Young Sinclair, pay attention! I'm going to have to depart. Perhaps you'll need me again sometime, to protect you from Kromer or something else. If you call me then, I will no longer come riding so crudely on a horse or on a train. Then you'll have to listen within yourself, and you'll notice that I'm inside you. Understand?—And one thing more! Lady Eve said that, if things ever went badly for you, I was to give you the kiss from her that she sent along with me... Close your eyes, Sinclair!"

I closed my eyes obediently; I felt a light kiss on my lips, on which there was always a little accumulation of blood that wouldn't decrease. And then I fell asleep.

In the morning I was awakened; I was to be bandaged. When I was finally properly awake, I turned over quickly toward the neighboring mattress. A stranger was lying on it, someone I'd never seen.

The bandaging hurt. Everything that has been done to me since then has hurt. But whenever I find the key at times, and descend all the way into myself, where the images of destiny slumber in the dark mirror, I need only lean over the black mirror to see my own image, which now looks exactly like him, him, my friend and guide.[9]

---

9. It has been suggested that the initial capital of Ihm in the German text indicates an identification of Demian with Christ. That may be, or it may merely indicate the same kind of emphasis the English translation conveys by italicizing "him."

Animal Farm

by George Orwell

Pages : 128 | ISBN : 9789354993381

Originally published in England in August 1945, 'Animal Farm' is a classic satire of the Russian Revolution by George Orwell, an English novelist, essayist, journalist, and critic. It is considered one of Orwell's most remarkable works, and a political fable based on the occurrences of Russia's Bolshevik Revolution and the betrayal of the cause by Joseph Stalin.

It is the account of the fierce struggle, initiated by the animals, that alters Mr. Jones's Manor Farm into Animal Farm, a wholly democratic society built on the ideology that "All Animals are Created Equal". Out of their intelligence, the pigs: Napoleon, Squealer, and Snowball materialize as leaders of the new community in a subtle evolution that proves disastrous. The pigs form a tyranny even more domineering and cruel than that of their former human masters.